Design
ON A
Crime

Other books by Ginny Aiken

Silver Hills Trilogy
Light of My Heart
Song of My Soul
Spring of My Love

Design ON A CRIME

DEADLY DÉCOR MYSTERIES
BOOK 1

Ginny Aiken

Revell
Grand Rapids, Michigan

© 2005 by Ginny Aiken

Published by Fleming H. Revell
a division of Baker Publishing Group
P.O. Box 6287, Grand Rapids, MI 49516-6287

Printed in the United States of America

Library of Congress Cataloging-in-Publication Data
Aiken, Ginny.
    Design on a crime / Ginny Aiken.
        p.   cm. — (Deadly decor mysteries; bk. 1)
    ISBN 0-8007-3044-5 (pbk.)
    1. Women interior decorators—Fiction. 2. Inheritance and succession—
Fiction. I. Title. II. Series: Aiken, Ginny. Deadly decor mysteries ; bk. 1.
PS3551.I339D47 2005
813′.54—dc22
                                         2005007750

Published in association with the literary agency of Alive Communications, Inc., 7680 Goddard Street, Suite 200, Colorado Springs, Colorado 80920.

He who began a good work in you will carry it on to completion until the day of Christ Jesus.

Philippians 1:6

1

Wilmont, Washington

When geriatric oak floorboards whine, wheeze, and creak their objection to a woman's presence, she should accept it as a sign that she's in for a rough ride. I instead glared at the testy wood. "Don't you dare give way . . ."

"Speaking to yourself?" Marge Norwalk asked.

I stumbled. The Gerrity mansion's century-old floor griped again. "I didn't hear you back there. You startled me."

"Lucky for me you didn't crouch and attack from one of your slice-and-dice martial arts positions."

"Lucky for you but lousy for me. I'm surprised I was so distracted."

"What's on your mind?"

"You have to ask?"

Marge placed a well-manicured hand on my shoulder. "Relax. Noreen's in the audience. She already signed for a bid paddle and even waved her checkbook at me. She intends hers to be the final bid—"

"That doesn't mean she'll hire me—"

"Stop." Marge's expression squashed further argument, so I let my mentor continue. "She assured me she would hire you because I endorsed your work. Over the years she's bought enough antiques from me to know I won't lead her astray on the choice of a decorator."

"Even one whose membership in the American Society of Interior Designers isn't dry on the books yet?"

"Even so."

The butterflies in my stomach chose that moment to morph into buzzards. Without this high-visibility job, my new business, Haley Farrell's Decorating $ense, didn't stand a chance. How could it?

Up until last week, when I hung out my oh-so-tasteful, gilt-lettered shingle over the mailbox at the Wilmont River Church's manse, I'd given away the fruits of my education in exchange for a lousy paycheck from a local furniture store. I consider the time I put in as a saleswoman at Rodgers and Faust Furnishings my requisite career purgatory. So do many others in my field.

But to go out on my own? Just on the encouragement of—more like kick in the butt from—Marge and the advice of the members of the church's missionary society?

"I still can't believe I let you badger me into quitting that job," I said. "Unemployment's a luxury I can't afford, and you know it. Dad still has a stack of Mom's medical bills to pay, and she's been gone for a year now. I can't make things harder for him."

Marge wagged a plum-nailed finger. "Now, Haley, is that any way for Pastor Hale Farrell's daughter to talk? Where's your faith, lady?"

Loss emptied my heart; a sour sensation filled my gut. Then, with determination, and before the memories had a chance to return in full Technicolor, I beat them back and turned to my tried-and-true friend, humor. "Hey, I'm a preacher's kid, don't ya know? We're the black sheep in the fold."

A frown pleated Marge's forehead. "More nightmares?"

Red rimmed the edge of my awareness. I shoved the bad stuff away again. "No more than usual. But let's not talk about it, okay? I think what I really need is another application of your infamous hobnailed boots to the hind side of my wimpy courage."

Marge's shoulders relaxed. "For a woman who's come as far as you have, I can't believe a little thing like the launch of your own business can turn you into such a sissy. Where's that killer instinct that made you a brown belt in . . ." She floundered for the name of a martial arts discipline. Then she waved. "A brown belt in whatever. If you can flip men three times your size onto their backs—"

"Only twice my size."

Marge swatted my shoulder. "Whatever. If you can lob behemoths without breaking a sweat, success in the business world's going to be a piece of cake. Remember, if I can do it, you can do it. Just picture difficult clients flat on their backs after you toss them."

"If you say so."

The sound system crackled to life. "Get going, Marge. Your adoring public awaits."

Marge wrinkled her nose, her chic wire-framed glasses bobbed, and she stepped toward the mansion's adjoining parlor and dining room, where the auction was set to take place. "You mean the status grubbers, don't you?"

"I don't think they all come to grub status. Tom and Gussie Stoker are here, and Gussie's a sweetheart with a passion for the past. The others from the missionary society just love the excitement of the bidding and always hope they can score a bargain or two."

Marge dipped her head. "You're right. They're not all bad—just most of them. You watch."

As Marge went to the podium, I scoured the room for Noreen Daventry's distinctive raven head. My—I hoped— future client is an attractive woman, one blessed with not only good looks but also a family fortune and a late husband whose death had made a generous contribution to the original kitty.

I found Noreen in the middle of the second row. She'd chosen the best seat in the house, the house she expected to own by the end of the day. The aisles were clotted with attendees scoping out the best seats before the sale. I excused myself to those already seated and, with the folds of my long green cotton dress clutched in one fist, I scooted toward my quarry.

Noreen turned up the power of her blue eyes in response to my hello. "I saved you a seat."

As I sat, I noticed the man to her left. I swallowed a groan.

Noreen draped an arm around the hunk's shoulders. "You know Dutch Merrill, don't you?"

"Not personally." I bent and tucked my black leather backpack purse under the chair to hide my reaction to Dutch.

None of what I know commends the guy. He graced the pages of the *Seattle Post-Intelligencer* on a regular basis over the last two years. A general contractor, he was taken to court when a house he built slid down one of Seattle's many hills in an extended heavy rain. Shoddy workmanship and substandard materials were alleged. The jury found him not guilty, but the verdict hasn't restored his reputation.

"Dutch," Noreen said in her lush, fudgy voice, "this is Haley Farrell, the interior designer Marge recommended. I'm glad you two can meet today, since I want you to work together on the remodel of my glorious new home." Her blue gaze touched every corner of the room.

Dutch nodded at me, then said to Noreen, "Aren't you counting unhatched chickens?"

"Not at all. I want this house."

As if that said it all. But since Noreen Daventry said it, I suppose it does say it all.

Dutch sat back, humming.

I choked down a laugh when I recognized the Rolling Stones' "You Can't Always Get What You Want." Maybe the shady builder wouldn't be so bad to work with. He had a sense of humor.

Just then, Marge clapped her gavel on the podium. "I can feel everyone's excitement this morning."

If she hadn't described the audience as status grubbers only minutes earlier, I'd never suspect that the elegant, thirty-nine-year-old businesswoman at the podium held anything but warm affection for them. I know where I stand with Marge; everyone who knows her does. Marge doesn't suffer fools, and she lets them know it.

The chatter died down to a low rumble. Marge went on. "Let's get started, shall we? We have a marvelous collection for sale today, and we begin with this turn of the century . . ."

When Marge's rapid-fire patter became pure gibberish, I gave up hope of following the bids. Paddles rose and fell at a furious pace. And the money some people will pay for pieces of . . . well, to be honest, junk? I can't believe it.

A couple of choice items did sell at a bargain, and I wished I had seed money to buy them. I can see the Gustav Stickley table as the focal point in a family room, and an excellent jewel-toned Kirman rug went for a song.

Noreen seemed to appreciate the advice I gave her on the dining room suite for twenty. The walnut table boasts an exquisite patina, developed over a century's application of rich oils, and the chairs, in spite of their hundred-plus years, still wear their original handworked tapestry. The sideboard and china cabinet are just as desirable. Noreen hovered around seventh heaven after her purchase.

That's when I took the time to check out the room. The six-foot-wide sideboard would look perfect against the dining room's left-hand wall, across from the Carrara marble fireplace. Placement of the massive china cupboard, though, would need more thought. The room's six windows eat up wall space, but I can't wait to dress them in dupioni silks—

Noreen's nails dug into my arm. "What do you think of that desk?"

Startled from my premature designs, I skimmed my auction catalog for the blurb beneath the photo of the piece. "I imagine it stood for years in the library. I see no reason to take it away, unless you don't win the house after . . . all . . ."

I let my voice die a slow death at Noreen's glare. "Which of course won't happen, since I know you'll get in the final bid and, no doubt, win."

I have to be way more careful. I can't afford to alienate my intense potential golden goose with my blunt tongue. Noreen means business, and anyone who crosses her, even by chance, stands to lose a limb or two.

Dutch leaned toward me and just missed a crash with Noreen's bid paddle. "Where do you plan to put that monstrosity of a china cupboard? Have you checked out all these windows? And don't forget the fireplace. I won't let you mess with perfection."

"You assume I would? I may be new to the business, but I know quality when I see it. That marble's not going anywhere—"

"Glad to hear it, but you didn't answer my question. What are you going to do with the walnut-and-glass white elephant?"

"Give it some thought, for one. I don't make snap decisions about a client's possessions. I specialize in carefully thought out, well-crafted designs and quality results."

His green eyes blazed. Bet he clicked on his memory's "save" icon at my barb. Oh well. There went my hope for a decent working relationship. I rubbed the raised embroidery on the skirt of my dress.

Noreen wriggled; her chair squeaked. "You were absolutely right, Haley. There's no reason in the world for that mahogany desk to leave its home. And now it won't have to."

I grimaced. Dutch had made me miss Noreen's purchase of the piece. I don't like the contractor any better now than when I first spotted him next to Noreen. That he'd managed to distract me from my responsibility to my client rubbed me the wrong way.

With Dutch in the picture, the redesign of the Gerrity mansion could easily become a greater challenge than I'd imagined. I'm not so sure I still wanted the job.

But I needed it.

I focused on Marge and thought only about the items that would work in the future décor of Noreen's maybe—hopefully—new house.

Hours later Noreen had racked up an eye-popping list of stuff. Acquisitiveness somewhat satisfied, she turned again to Dutch. I couldn't help but notice how good they looked together. In a masculine way, Dutch is as beautiful as Noreen, and he makes an excellent foil for her. Was there more than just business between them? Was he the builder with whom Marge said she thought Noreen was involved?

It seemed the only conceivable reason for Noreen, who can hire anyone she wants, to turn to Dutch of the shady track record.

"For this stunning beauty," Marge said moments later, a crystal and silver epergne in her hands, "the last item in our catalog, we'll start the bidding at a bargain two hundred and fifty dollars."

Paddles flashed from every corner of the room. Marge's chatter became mush to my unenlightened ears. Finally, in understandable English, she asked, "Twelve fifty? Do we have twelve fifty for this perfect piece?"

No one moved.

With a flourish, Marge handed the epergne to her longtime assistant, Oswald Krieger. "Fair warning," she sang out.

When no other bid materialized, she smacked the podium with the gavel. "Sold! To number 321 for twelve hundred dollars."

The audience sighed. Rented metal chairs squealed as bidders relaxed.

Marge added, "Are you ready for a break?"

A collective yes sissed forth.

"Well, then, how about twenty minutes? I'm looking forward to the sale of this grand old home. I hope you are too." Marge winked. "And may the best man—or woman—win!"

I stood, stretched discreetly, and extricated myself from the center of the row. After I stepped on a number of feet and apologized to their owners, I burst from the dining room into the parlor and then out of the house. My goal was the nearest of the putty-colored port-a-potties that mushroomed up along the right edge of the lawn.

After much-needed relief, I strolled to the tent where Marge's favorite caterer had set out a cold lunch. The auction business pays well. Marge shares the wealth, but only by hiring the best. Still, her clients appreciate the gesture and the excellent, if pricey, food. They repay with their attendance and purchases at all her sales.

Delicious turkey on grainy bread and pasta salad hit the spot, and soon after, I headed back to the house. But my return to my seat was foiled by a gaggle of Dad's parishioners who ambushed me in the foyer. The ladies of the missionary society like their auctions.

"Isn't she marvelous?" Ina Appleton asked.

I assumed she meant Marge. "I've always thought so."

An arm circled my waist. "As are you," Gussie Stoker said.

"Thanks." I hugged her back. Gussie's advanced rheumatoid arthritis keeps her in constant pain, hampers her movements, and gives her a much older appearance than her fifty years of age. I took some of her weight on my healthy frame.

"Humph!" You could always count on Penelope Harham, Wilmont's postal clerk, to dissent. As usual, her sniff wasn't enough. "Haley is utterly unqualified to preside over the missionary society, Gussie Stoker, and you know it."

I fought the urge to roll my eyes. "I'm ready to step down, Penny, and I told you that last week."

"You'll do no such thing," Gussie retorted.

"Why not let her?" Penny demanded. "It's obvious she lacks the most basic commitment to the job. Everyone knows she was chosen only because of your strong-arm tactics."

Against my loud and repeated objection, the charitable ladies, led by Gussie, their interim president, have elected me as their leader. They've proclaimed me the rightful successor to Mom's favorite position. Not wanting to cause dissension in Dad's congregation, I accepted the post but keep my eyes and ears open for the first chance to run.

"Honestly, Gussie—"

"Honestly, Haley. You're the right woman for the job."

"I don't know about that, not now that I've rejoined the ranks of the unemployed. I have to drum up business for Decorating $ense. I can't be sure Noreen's going to wind up with the house, much less hire me as she said she would. I don't have a lot of time for meetings and stuff."

"Even if Noreen doesn't buy the house, you don't need to worry." Gussie eased slowly back into her wheelchair. "Tom and I have wanted to do something about our living and dining rooms for a while now. We decided you're the perfect person for our job."

One half of me wanted to decline the Stokers' charity, but the other half wanted to do a touchdown dance at my first real designer gig. In the end, I did neither, but rather moved the wheelchair a couple of feet to give my champion a better view of the podium. "Okay, Gussie. I'll do it. I won't let you down."

"That's why you're about to become the top designer in the state of Washington. And I'm not biased."

"Nah, of course you aren't." I grinned. "You're just a wild gambler at heart."

I scanned the crowd for Tom Stoker. At my nod, he left the men with whom he'd been talking and came to take over the wheelchair again. "Thanks, Haley."

"Don't mention it. I love Gussie."

"We all do. But I still appreciate your help."

"You're welcome." I turned to look for Noreen. She was still where I'd left her, surrounded by a swarm of bidders, deep in conversation with Dutch. I headed over.

A brown dervish spun into my path. "Have you seen Margaret?" Ozzie Krieger asked.

"Not since she called for an intermission. Why?"

"Because, Miss Farrell, I cannot locate her."

"And . . . ?"

"And she is quite late."

"I'm sure she's on her way. Just relax and give her a minute or two."

"I have already given her ten more than she requested."

My watch said thirty minutes had passed since the gavel had brought the bidding to an end. Marge had called for twenty, and Marge is always on time.

Ozzie's left eyebrow twitched, and he wrung his hands. "Do you now understand what I mean? Margaret never leaves except to go to the—" he glanced around and blushed "—latrine. She has had more than sufficient time to return. This isn't in any way like her."

Much though I hated to agree with the nebbish Ozzie, Marge's delay was unusual. I hadn't been to many auctions, but Marge and I had talked about her complete concentration at sales. She rarely took time out for lunch; she'd never disappear for half an hour.

"Tell you what, Ozzie. I'll help you look for her."

The slender man's pinched expression didn't change. "I'm much obliged, Miss Farrell. If you would please take the house, then I shall check outside again."

In those few minutes, Ozzie infected me with his anxiety. I ran up the majestic staircase to the gallery above.

"Marge? Are you up here?"

When I got no answer, I opened every door. The rooms were empty. I repeated my efforts on the third floor with the same unfortunate results.

Back on the ground floor, I asked a number of people if they'd seen Marge. No one had.

My anxiety shifted into worry. Where was Marge?

It occurred to me that Ozzie might have missed his boss in the crowded food tent. I headed out again, but instead of cutting straight across the lawn, I detoured around the perimeter of the columned house. Maybe Marge had needed a break. The intensity had to get to her sometimes, and this was a major sale.

A bright sun in the clear blue sky belied the bad rap the Seattle area gets for its weather. True, it had rained earlier in the day, but all that had done was clean the world and leave it luminous and fresh scented.

I breathed deep and savored the essence of my hometown. The perfume of sea-salty air mixed with the aroma of living soil, then tangled with the spice of the ubiquitous evergreens. No other place on earth smells like Wilmont, Seattle, and the Puget Sound. Not that I've traveled much to test my conviction. My quirky bias made me grin.

I rounded the corner and went around the back of the mansion. That part of the house had a quilt of vegetation tucked in around the brick foundation. A vast elephant fern frond blocked my way. I had to push hard to move the greenery aside. "Marge?"

All I got for my effort was a sprinkle of raindrops from that morning's shower. I continued to pick my way around the landscaping. My shoes sank into the loamy ground.

"Marge? Where are you?"

Still no answer.

Then I saw it. A stain the color of Cherry Coke stood out against the grass at the base of a massive rhododendron. My worry congealed into fear, and I fought the urge to run.

I couldn't leave. Not until I knew what had made the stain. And found Marge.

I bent for a closer look at the spot. A rusty, copper smell muddied the fresh tang of the Pacific Northwest.

My heart pounded, but I pressed on. To one side and behind the rhododendron, another heavy fern got in my way. But between its wavy leaves, I spied a sliver of plum.

My stomach turned.

When I shoved that frond out of my way, I moaned. Marge lay under the shrubbery, her head in an ocean of her own blood.

2

Darkness yawned, and a pit swallowed me. Sweat drenched me. Horror made me frantic. I fell, reached for a handhold, grabbed a rock. A weird, high-pitched sound pierced the fog around me. It took me a couple of seconds to recognize the screams as mine. Ozzie materialized and joined his moans to my cries.

I willed myself to stop. I shut my eyes tight, hugged myself. None of it helped. The image of Marge burned in my mind.

A crowd formed around Ozzie and me, and in spite of my misery, I had the sense to warn them. "Move back. Call the police."

"Do you think she's . . ." I recognized the woman's voice but couldn't identify her right then.

"Have you touched her?" a man asked.

"Is that blood?" someone else wanted to know.

My stomach lurched. My whole body shuddered. The tremors reached my fingers, and they shook like leaves in a gale.

"I . . ." My throat shut out my words.

"She asked you to move back, didn't she?" a third man

asked. I recognized that voice too but couldn't place it either. "From where I'm standing," he added, "Mrs. Norwalk looks dead, and Ms. Farrell and Mr. Krieger need room. Move back!"

I clenched my fists, blinked over and over. I didn't feel any better, but I did catch a glimpse of a tall, muscular man, his broad chest covered with a polo shirt the color of his green eyes.

He pulled a cell phone from his belt, pushed some buttons, and then spoke. He nodded, flipped the gadget shut, and tucked it back in place. With a glare at a curious woman in acid yellow, he knelt at my side, cupped my elbow, helped me sit then stand.

"They're on their way," he said. "At least Wilmont's small. They'll be here in minutes." To the gawkers, he added, "The police dispatcher asked that everyone return to the parlor and dining room. We're not to speak to each other or touch anything, and no one can leave."

He turned to Noreen. "Find the security guy. I don't see him anywhere, and he should have shown up at Haley's first yell."

The welcome wail of a siren struck me as perfect punctuation for his words. Noreen's glare, now that she was at the other end of an order, made things click back to reality for me. Dutch Merrill's take-charge attitude bugged Noreen; he'd trampled her authoritarian toes.

On the other hand, I appreciated his intervention. Without his grip on my arm, I'd have quivered back to the ground at Marge's side. I felt that weak.

I hated it.

To get out of Dutch's grip, I had to use the strength I'd developed in four years of martial arts training. "I'm fine."

The guard ran up. "Wha . . . what happened?"

Dutch pointed to where Marge lay. "And where were you?"

With a bluster and a blush to the roots of his disappearing hairline, the man said, "I . . . well, you see . . ." He hitched up his khaki uniform pants, then stared at the sky. "I had to use the . . . john, and the latch stuck . . ."

Grover Potter, as per his badge, bit his bottom lip. He turned to me. "Begging pardon, ma'am."

My smile wasn't worth much, but at least it showed up. I felt sorry for him, for Marge. For me. A tear rolled down my cheek. I swiped it away and fought down the sob before it got out.

My closest friend, the person who knew me best, was dead. I didn't need to get any closer to the body to know Marge's essence was gone.

As soon as I stepped away from Dutch, chills riddled me. By now the shivers weren't so bad, but the frozen sensation felt as though it had come to stay.

From what sounded like a great distance, I heard Dutch say, "She found Mrs. Norwalk."

I clamped down on my emotions and listened. The police had come. When an officer knelt by Marge, I nearly chased him away. It felt like an insult for anyone to see her like that, damaged, broken.

But the man had a job to do.

I looked around. At Dutch's right stood a petite Asian woman, her dark hair gathered in a sleek knot at the nape of her neck. Her rose-colored suit matched the simple elegance of her hairstyle, while the frown on her pretty face seemed out of place.

With a glance, the woman put me under a microscope.

Since the best defense is always a good offense, I extended my hand. "Haley Farrell. I came outside to look for Marge when she didn't show up after the intermission. I found her just as she is. Nobody disturbed her, although I can't vouch for the lawn. When I screamed, everyone came running. I'm sorry about the footprints."

The woman's hand was as cool and smooth as her appearance. "I'm Lila Tsu," she said. "Detective with the Wilmont PD. I'll be heading the investigation."

I nodded.

The detective continued. "You need to go back inside. We'll take statements from everyone, but we have to secure the area first. We also have to wait for the coroner. Since Wilmont isn't big enough for us to have our own, it will take him some time to get through the Seattle traffic."

I nodded again.

Detective Tsu's eyes narrowed. "Remember, Ms. Farrell, you can't speak to anyone. I understand it's hard to wait in silence, but it's in your best interest to do so."

Did she think I wanted to while away my afternoon with Marge's clients? I gave a third brief nod and, now mostly numb, headed for the house. When I reached the columned front porch, I heard a hiss.

"Over here, Miss Farrell."

"Ozzie! What are you doing? The police asked everyone to go inside."

"I've been waiting for you, miss. I must ask—"

"Don't say anything else. We're not supposed to talk."

Ozzie's eyes bulged. He looked about to burst. Someone else to feel sorry for. I knew how much I wanted—needed—to talk to someone about what I'd found, what I'd seen. But cops mean business.

I patted Ozzie's shoulder, then led him inside. Unnatural silence filled rooms that a short while ago had hummed with excitement. As I looked for an empty chair, I saw a policeman scribble in a small notebook. At his side, Penny Harham whispered and nodded sagaciously.

Great. If the cops relied on her, they'd never learn what happened to Marge. Penny's vision of reality is hers and hers alone.

Hours trickled by in itchy silence. The lousy metal chair made my back hurt. Some rows back, a man gave in to fatigue, and his snores kept the rest of us wide awake. Finally, Detective Tsu appeared with the officer who'd spoken to Penny. Just like that, the atmosphere changed.

I sat up. Maybe we'd all get sent home soon. Dad was probably wondering what had happened to me. I'd told him I'd be home no later than two o'clock, and it was going on five by now.

"If I could have your attention," Detective Tsu said. "Because there are so many of you, we're going to take down names and addresses and contact you at home."

Relief rustled through the crowd.

"Wait," cautioned the detective, her hand up like a traffic cop's. "Some of you will still need to stay." Her needle gaze skewered me. "Since Ms. Farrell and Mr. Krieger were the first on the scene, I'll need them to stay. Those who live outside the

Seattle area will also have to wait for us to get to you today. And if anyone has information that might help, please don't wait for us to ask. Tell us now."

My hope for a quick return home flapped away on the wings of a musical but steely voice.

Soon that voice peppered me with more questions than I'd ever thought any one person could ask. Everything from my education to Marge's favorite foods was fair game.

Exhaustion took its toll; my answers took a turn down Cranky Lane.

Detective Tsu didn't like the trip. "I understand this is tedious, but a woman lost her life—"

"You don't have to tell me. I found her. And she means—" My voice broke. I tried again. "She *meant* a lot to me. I've told you all I know. Most of your questions have nothing to do with anything, at least not with what I saw today." Hysteria sprouted. "Can I please go home?"

Ms. Tsu checked her watch, then scanned the room and nodded to the officer by the door. He hurried over. "They're waiting."

"I guess we can wrap it up for tonight." The elegant detective turned off her pocket recorder. "We'll be in touch again, Ms. Farrell. Even without the necessary autopsy, it's obvious Mrs. Norwalk was murdered, and since you found the victim, we will have more questions for you."

She put her notebook, silver-toned pen, and recorder in a square leather purse. She slanted me another laser look. "You'll need to identify the body before you leave."

"Me? Why? Everyone saw Marge. Everyone knows who died. Why do I have to . . . to see . . . her again?"

Bile jetted up my throat. I didn't want to look at that empty shell under the shrubs again. I wanted to remember my mentor as the vibrant woman I'd known for years. I didn't want to face that lifeless, spiritless . . . thing another time.

Detective Tsu remained implacable. "The coroner needs a formal identification."

"Can't Ozzie do it?" I was desperate. "How about Steve? Steve Norwalk, Marge's husband."

"Officer Young is still taking Mr. Krieger's statement, and Mr. Norwalk is out of town. It won't take but a minute, Ms. Farrell. You said you wanted to leave, so please come with us. You can go home afterward."

I grabbed my backpack purse and stood. I could do this. I could. If I'd made it through the last four years, then I'd also survive this.

"Fine," I said.

My steps echoed in the empty rooms.

Outside, I rounded a corner and went to the backyard. A yellow ribbon screamed "Crime Scene" and added to the surreal quality of the lavender dusk. I slowed down as I approached three men around what looked like a lumpy bag.

I gagged.

I can do it. I can do it.

"Here's Ms. Farrell," Detective Tsu said.

A nondescript gentleman in a short-sleeved plaid shirt and new-looking jeans knelt by the lump and ripped the zipper open. "Come closer."

I bit my lip. Marge's blond hair, wire-rimmed glasses, high

forehead, straight nose, and wide mouth were there. Marge wasn't.

"What do you want me to say?"

"Identify the body, please," the man said.

"It *was* Marge Norwalk. It's an empty body now." Nausea swelled. "I have to go. Please."

My Honda Civic had never seemed so far away. I ran, gulped down evening air, prayed I wouldn't vomit and humiliate myself. I don't know how I made it to the relative safety of my car.

By virtue of sheer cussed determination, I didn't hit anything on the way home. On autopilot, I parked in the manse's driveway, locked the car, and ran up the front steps. A light shone in the living room. The strains of Pachelbel's "Canon" reached out through the open window.

I was home.

But would I ever be safe?

"Haley?" Dad called out.

Every bone in my body melted at the sound of that much-loved voice. I stumbled in. "Yeah, I'm home. I'm so . . . sorry . . . I'm late . . ."

Sobs stole my voice. Dad wrapped his arms around me and pulled me close. He led me to the sofa, where he continued to hold me. He rocked me like he had when I was little. I wished I still were. Then what I'd seen wouldn't be real. I wouldn't have had to go through it.

But I wasn't a child. The pain told me I hadn't imagined a thing. And I hadn't explained my anguish to Dad.

In a guttural croak, I said, "Marge is dead."

My father closed his eyes. His lips moved in prayer. My

tears flowed on, silent now. As they did for the rest of the night.

The phone rang me awake only moments after I finally fell asleep. At least, that was how I felt. I reached for the miserable machine. "Wilmont River Church manse, Haley speaking."

"They canceled the auction," Dutch growled.

"And a very good morning to you too." His words registered. I reeled from the fresh flood of images and fell back against the pillows. "They? The auction?"

"Yes, Haley, the auction. The sale of the Gerrity mansion was called off. By the police. Because it was the scene of a crime, they sealed the property and postponed the sale indefinitely."

"Gee. Thanks for the news. Tell me again why you felt the need to share with me."

"Because according to the morning paper, you're about to become filthy rich. And your fingerprints and footprints were all over the place. That big inheritance gives you an awfully good reason to want Mrs. Norwalk dead, doesn't it?"

This had to be a nightmare. It made no sense.

He made no sense.

"What are you talking about? And why are you yelling at me?"

"Inheritance, Haley." I heard him fight for control. Then his words came out measured, careful. "I'm talking about Marge Norwalk's will. The one where she cuts her husband out without a penny. According to her lawyer, you get everything, even the auction house. The same auction house the Gerrity heirs hired to sell the matriarch's mansion. Marge's lawyer leaked the details. It's all in the *Seattle Times* for you to read."

My head spun. The world had tilted out of orbit at the Gerrity the day before, and it refused to settle back down. "I'm sure there's some kind of mistake. I know nothing about Marge's will or any newspaper story. All I know is that my friend died a horrible death yesterday."

"Your friend isn't the only casualty, you know."

"Oh?"

"The renovation of that mansion means a great deal to me, and a murder investigation means trouble. I need that job, and the killer is responsible for the delay."

My temper began a slow boil. "You know, Dutch Merrill, you give one fabulous condolence call. On top of that, your insinuations are offensive, and you're making me mad. I've never hurt anybody, especially not Marge. And I resent—"

"*I* resent your interfering with Marge's life, and as a result, mine. I'm as sorry as the next guy about her death. She seemed okay. But she's gone, and you have the best motive for wanting her dead. Plus, your fingerprints put you at the scene. I can't afford to let your greed keep me from getting on with my life."

"Now, you listen to me—"

"No, *you* listen to *me*. I'm going to do everything in my power to help the cops nail the killer so Noreen can buy the Gerrity. The sooner the better. And from where I sit, lady, you're it."

"It? You're nuts. I have nothing to gain from Marge's death. You don't know what you're saying."

Tears poured again, but I fought the sobs with everything I had. I refused to give this wacko a glimpse into my grief.

I went on. "I don't want her money or her company or her stuff—I never did. I want her friendship, her kindness . . . even her lectures. But now she's gone, and I have nothing left. How dare you—"

"Can the drama. I don't buy it. I'm going to watch every step you take. You watch. At the first mistake, I'll have the cops all over you faster than you can sneeze."

He killed the call with a slam.

3

I stared at the phone. That had to hold the Nobel prize for worst wake-up call. "He's out of his sleazy, corner-cutting, cheap, and shoddy mind," I muttered. I needed to hear something, even my own rant about the disturbing dolt.

"Now there's a word for you," I added when Midas licked my chin. "*Disturbing*. As in disturbed. As in Dutch Merrill is one disturbed character."

The saddest eyes in creation, that unique, heart-tug brown gaze of the golden retriever, followed me as I stood, dug out clean underwear, jeans, and a T-shirt from my blue milk-painted chest of drawers, then made a beeline for the shower. Doggy nails clicked against hardwood floors, a comforting, familiar sound.

"Haley?" Dad called from downstairs.

"Yeah?"

"Who was that?"

Dutch's rugged good looks flashed through my mind. Too bad he's certifiable. What a waste. "Just a wrong number." *Boy, did he ever have the wrong number. To accuse me—me!*

"Oh. Okay."

The scent of cinnamon wafted up from below. My mouth watered.

Dad added, "There's coffee, and the apple muffins just came out of the oven."

Love and guilt mingled. When he has something on his mind, Dad bakes. His apple muffins constitute a major food group all their own—just like Starbucks fine roasts and Milky Way bars. As he tried to comfort himself, he'd comfort me too.

"I'll be right down." I started the shower. Dad knows how much Marge meant to me. He'd always encouraged our friendship, even more in the last few years.

I frothed a glob of coconut-scented shampoo between my palms and scrubbed my scalp. I'd be pretty happy if I could wash away the trash life dumped on me as easily as I could suds out grime.

A slimeball nearly did me in four years ago, and by extension, Mom and Dad too. They'd clung to their faith and waited for miraculous healing. I, on the other hand, couldn't. What the sicko did to me killed my faith.

Marge listened to my angry screams. She sat through the joke the law called a trial. She even stuffed me into her immaculate vintage VW Beetle, then dumped me back out at Tyler Colby's *dojo*.

Thanks to Tyler's no-nonsense approach to martial arts and Marge's use of her proverbial hobnailed boots, I crawled out of my pit of despair, inch by ugly inch. In time, Dad talked me into going back to school, but I couldn't see myself as a future accountant anymore. The neatness of numbers and equations had nothing to do with life. They sure didn't make it more logical.

After hours spent with Marge at her auction house's warehouse, I decided to check out interior design as a career. It held the promise of freedom in self-employment. I wanted to work for myself as soon as I could. Authority and power are now impossible to accept as blindly as I once did. They remind me how weak I was, how helpless, at the mercy of the merciless.

Design has an extra bonus for my battered psyche. It surrounds me with and helps me focus on beauty rather than on the random acts of ugliness that happen every day.

I turned off the shower and squeezed excess water from my hair. I twisted the whole long mess of it in a soft blue Egyptian cotton towel and wrapped myself in another.

Steam fogged the beveled mirror over the vanity. Good. After yesterday, not to mention Dutch's call, I didn't want to see my eyes. I didn't want to find the misery I'd seen there before.

Midas whined out in the hall. I'd taken too long for him. He wanted my company, and he wanted it now.

I hurried into my clothes. "I'm coming."

The wide-toothed comb snagged in my crazy, wavy brown hair a bunch of times, but eventually, I had the damp mess spread over my shoulders. I hoped it would dry fast; I held out no hope for neat or anything less than wild. I hurried to join my dog.

I rubbed his head. "You want one of those muffins too, don't you? Sorry."

Midas struck a defiant pose, feet squared beneath his silky furred chest, and *woo-woo-wooed* back.

"Tough. You can't have one. They're lousy for you. I'll give you a nice, big bowl of Eukanuba's best instead."

Downstairs I opened the metal bin of premium kibble and scooped Midas's breakfast into his dish. The Golden One was not amused. Powerful body braced before the food, Midas glared from the brown pellets to me and back again. His feathered tail whipped the air; his body broadcast displeasure.

"Hey, that's life. 'You can't always get what you want—'"

I caught myself. Terrific. Dutch's song from the auction. What did that say about me? After all, the guy wasn't all there.

How could he think I'd killed Marge? Even the police weren't that dumb. Detective Tsu of the feminine elegance and sharp gaze had said I was an important witness. After all, I did find Marge. Only a paranoid fruitcake would twirl that in his warped little brain and come up pointing fingers.

Dad came into the kitchen and shuffled canisters on the counters. "Have you seen my reading glasses? I had them when I did a crossword a little while ago, but I can't figure out where they went after that."

I grinned. Some things never change. "Check your shirt pocket."

"Aha!" He put on the half-moons and winked over the frames. "I knew you'd find them." At the back door, he added, "I'll be at the office, but if you need me, just call. I don't have anything so urgent on my schedule that I can't beg off. Sunday's sermon's written. This—" he gestured vaguely "—is going to be tough on you."

"And on you. Marge was a good friend to you and Mom for years."

"True, very true." He shook his head. "These last few have been rough, haven't they?"

Pain swelled in my throat.

"Faith, honey," Dad said, even though he knew how I felt. "The Lord will see us through."

Maybe you, but he hasn't done a thing for me. "I'll call if I need you."

Once he left I helped myself to a mug of Starbucks House Blend and a muffin. In spite of the scrumptious scents, I couldn't even nibble.

What would life be like without Marge?

If I hadn't had to take that second, horrible look at her lifeless body, I would probably be trying to assure myself that the whole horrible day had been a nightmare. But it had been too real. I couldn't question my memory.

Marge was dead.

Someone had hated her enough to kill her.

Or maybe that someone had resented her strength, her success. It doesn't matter why they did it. What matters is that Marge is gone.

I can't imagine hurting anyone or anything. Except maybe banana slugs and spiders. They gross me out. But the thought of violence, doing real, vicious harm, is beyond me. Even memories of my very own slimeball don't send me into a kill-crazy frenzy. And he *did* hurt me.

What makes people turn violent?

Before I could come up with any answer, the phone rang.

"Haley Farrell?"

"Yes. How may I help you?"

"Sam Harris here. Margaret Norwalk's attorney. By now I'm sure you've read the papers and must be wondering what's up."

I rapped my nails against the tabletop. "Actually, Mr. Harris, I made it a point to avoid them. A rude and offensive phone call this morning informed me that you cozied up to the press last night. What did you think you'd gain by blabbing before poor Marge's body had the chance to get stiff?"

Harris cleared his throat. "This is a criminal matter, Ms. Farrell. I had to cooperate with the police."

Nice try, buddy. "Cops don't write newspapers. Since when does cooperation mean you spill clients' private matters to the whole wide world? Ever hear of attorney-client privilege?"

"Look. You may not like it, but it's done."

"Just like Marge is dead, and I don't like it. Is that it?"

Silence. Then, "I called to ask you to come to my office at your earliest convenience. I have Marge's will, and I need to give you a copy."

"Then it's true?"

"You're Marge Norwalk's heir."

Still disgusted by the ambulance chaser's unethical actions, I agreed to meet him that afternoon, then hung up.

What would it mean to be Marge's heir? The Farrell family has never had much money. True, the church pays its pastor an acceptable salary, and here in Wilmont the manse comes along as part of his compensation. But Marge had real money, a lot of it. Her business is successful, and she knew how to invest for the best return.

"Hey, Midas. Isn't that something? I'm going to have a savings account with a balance. Investments. Even an auction house. Imagine that."

My stomach lurched. "And I don't know a thing about auctions. I'm just a brand-spanking-new interior designer.

All I want is to make people's homes and offices look good. What am I going to do with Marge's stuff?"

By the time I left Sam Harris's office hours later, I'd worked up a killer headache and more questions than I'd had when I arrived. No answers though.

The only additional thing I'd learned was the size of Marge's healthy portfolio, hefty life-insurance policy, and humongous certificates of deposit. Oh, and her business was making a bundle too.

From what Harris led me to believe, as soon as probate was complete, I'd have access to all that money, even though Steve Norwalk threatened to contest the will. Something told me shady shysters knew how to write airtight wills . . . something about the color of money.

Memories of yesterday's antiques returned on the drive home from downtown Seattle. It looked as though I'd soon have the seed money I'd wished for during the auction. Maybe I could rent a store for Decorating $ense. A showroom would be great, stocked with quality pieces, a mix of old and new. I'd set them up in roomlike groups so clients could draw ideas from the settings. Racks of fabric swatches would help, as would a section of wallpaper books, a separate room for salvaged architectural details, and even paint chips and assorted wood-finish samples. Marge would be so proud—

No, she wouldn't. Marge wasn't going to be around. Tears filled my eyes, and misery squeezed my heart.

For once, the legendary traffic snarls on I-5 didn't faze me. I was too absorbed in my own thoughts, and then I had to handle a tough condolence call from a friend. But when I

finally reached my exit, I did manage a watery smile. The narrow streets of Wilmont, lined with old and not-so-old homes,
were far more appealing than the bumper-to-bumper gleam
on one of the country's most congested roadways.

Then I turned onto Puget Way. Warm fuzzies usually hit
me at the first glimpse of home. But what I saw kicked the
sick reality of yesterday's tragedy up to life again.

A Wilmont PD cruiser sat in the driveway behind Dad's
car. I made out two heads in the front seat, one of which
belonged to Detective Tsu.

I pasted on a pseudogrin to approach the official vehicle.
"I assume you're waiting for me."

The front passenger-side door opened. The detective, today
in a cream linen trousers suit, stepped out. I shook the cool
hand she extended and couldn't stop the comparison between
its softness and my own warm, sweaty, dishwater-and-paint-
thinner-rough mitt.

"As I said yesterday," Ms. Tsu said, "we have more questions for you."

"I didn't doubt it. Come in."

Ms. Tsu sat on the shabby-chic white-slip-covered sofa, and
I took Mom's rocker. The little tape recorder came out of the
detective's glam black purse, and she began.

"We have a list of everyone who attended the auction.
But before I show it to you, I want you to name anyone you
remember. On your own."

I felt we were about to play a tricky little game, one where
someone somewhere had the odds stacked against me. I
named Marge, Ozzie, Noreen, and Dutch, then ran down a
list of the members of the missionary society. "Some of the

ladies planned to bring their spouses, but I don't remember any besides Tom Stoker. I didn't pay much attention to the others. I was there on business."

Ms. Tsu wove her silver pen through the fingers of her right hand. "Tell me about your business."

"There's not a whole lot to tell. I quit my sales job at Rodgers and Faust three weeks ago and took out ads in the local newspapers and the two Seattle biggies to launch Decorating $ense last week. Noreen Daventry asked me to join her at the Gerrity auction. She wanted my professional opinion on a slew of things she liked and for me to look at the house. She's decided to buy it and have me design the décor."

The detective dipped her smooth-coiffed head to her left. "That must represent a substantial commission, right?"

"You bet. The Gerrity mansion's well known. Whoever brings it back will earn a good chunk of change. And besides the commission, that job will mean the best kind of publicity. Noreen—Ms. Daventry—entertains all the time. Once her guests check out the house, her designer'll get a bunch of referrals."

"So it's in your best interest for the sale to go through."

"Of course."

"What does the delay mean to you?"

What was she, stupid? But her dark eyes nixed that possibility. "It means I'm the owner of a sign over my mailbox. Without the sale, Noreen can't hire me. I'm unemployed."

Ms. Tsu cocked her head to the right. She scanned her notebook. "Hmm . . . I have here that Mr. and Mrs. Thomas Stoker hired you to redo their living and dining rooms. Why did you say you're unemployed?"

"I forgot. Gussie asked me right before Ozzie—Mr. Krieger—came and asked me to help him find Marge. You should be able to figure out how Gussie's rooms might have slipped my mind."

"But you still need Ms. Daventry's job, right?"

"Oh yeah."

"So the auctioneer's death doesn't benefit you."

"I never gave it a thought until this morning when . . ." The thought of the phone call riled my temper.

Detective Tsu's voice sliced through my rising anger. "When what, Ms. Farrell?"

Great. I'd practically waved a red flag at the cop. "Please call me Haley." Amiable coexistence would be good, but I didn't think it had a chance. "I've a feeling we're going to see a lot of each other for a while."

Ms. Tsu looked up, the corner of her rose-glossed lips tipped into the slightest smile. "I'm afraid you're right. But go on. What happened this morning?"

"Dutch Merrill called to land a couple of low blows. The guy's certifiable. He accused me of all kinds of outrageous things."

When I paused, Ms. Tsu asked, "What kind of things?"

"He accused me of—" my voice broke "—of killing Marge."

The detective didn't react. "Why would he do that?"

"He read this morning's paper. Marge's scumbag lawyer fed the details of her will to the *Times*."

"And those details are . . . ?"

My patience was shot. "Don't treat me like an idiot, Ms. Tsu, and I won't underestimate you. You couldn't have missed

the news, even if you hadn't already talked to Sam Harris.
I'm Marge Norwalk's heir. Dutch thinks I killed her to get
my hands on her money."

The silver pen danced on among the rose-tipped fingers.
The sunlight pouring in through the front window sparkled
off its shiny metal sides.

I stood and paced. Talk of Marge's death brought back the
gut-wrenching misery of last night. Dutch's call just made
me mad. The collision of emotions made me itch to go break
some bricks, kick a punching bag, sweat out my pain while I
strengthened my body. I couldn't stand to feel weak.

Helpless.

I faced the still-silent detective. "I didn't know Marge
planned to leave me anything, much less everything. I thought
Merrill was delusional when he called."

"You don't anymore, do you?"

I raised my arms in exasperation. "How could I? After
the charming chat with Contractor Cheat, I got a call from
Barrister Blither. I went into Seattle and was on my way back
when I found you in my driveway. Mr. Harris gave me a copy
of the will. It's all true."

"So now things have changed."

I pushed a bunch of hair behind my ear. In the presence of
the *Vogue* model detective, I regretted not taking the time to
try to corral my rowdy mane. "I'll say."

"A dead Marge benefits you more than a live Marge,
wouldn't you also say?"

I stared down the detective's hazel eyes. "No, Detective
Tsu, I would not say that. Marge means—meant—a lot more
to me yesterday than her money does today. I can't believe

anyone would think anything else. Especially you. Detectives are supposed to be rational, guided by evidence and facts. This was just the ranting of a paranoid maniac."

"Merrill?"

"Yes."

The detective's gaze didn't waver when she closed her notebook. "We haven't spoken with him since yesterday at the mansion."

My gut knotted up. "Does this mean that Wilmont's PD now operates on flights of fantasy?"

"Hardly. As you just said, we—I—operate on evidence and fact."

"Then you can't be serious. You can't think I killed Marge. You can't have any evidence, since I didn't do it."

Ms. Tsu clicked off her recorder. She stood, her posture perfect, her stance assured. She seemed taller than before, and her poise again impressed me.

"That's where I'm afraid you're wrong, Ms. Farrell. We have evidence that places you at the scene."

My heart thudded. I rolled my eyes. "About four hundred people saw me there. Remember? I'm the one who found Marge."

"Yes, Ms. Farrell. That would account for your footprints. But how do you account for your fingerprints on the rock that crushed Marge Norwalk's skull?"

With the speed of a crashing gavel, blackness crushed me.

4

The next morning, when I walked into the *dojo*, Tyler wore his usual smile on his face and X-ray vision in his eyes. He reached out to hug me. "Hey there, girl. What brings you here during the day?"

"Unemployment."

"What do you mean? I thought you'd just opened your new business."

"I did. But a funny thing happened on my way to stardom and success. Those in the know call it murder one."

My *sensei* narrowed his intense dark eyes. "You're going to have to tell me more than that."

"Can we just not talk about it? I really need to kick something."

For a moment, I thought he'd refuse to let me get away with my dodge, but I wasn't ready to rehash the last two days. Then his eyes took a trip over my whacked-out, grief-stricken self.

"Okay. Take your time."

I'd have my moment of reckoning soon enough. I'd known I would, but even though I wished I didn't have to, at least

Tyler would give me time and space to get myself together again.

Marge was the one who'd made sure I could in the recent past. Even though I felt rotten already, I knew the full reality of her death hadn't hit me yet. The coward in me wanted to run, but I knew I could only postpone that moment.

Time to sweat. This was the place to do it.

Tyler teaches his own mongrel mix of disciplines. For endurance and flexibility, he has his students learn Tai Chi; for strength, he favors Tae Kwan Do; for power, jujutsu; for self-defense, down and dirty kickboxing.

I changed into a white *gi*, tied on my brown belt, and hurried to join the class about to start. I had no idea which discipline was on the menu, but I figured I'd take a serving of any of them. I hoped for kickboxing.

Two women in their late fifties told me we'd be doing Tai Chi. A seemingly easy and slow martial art, Tai Chi is a lot more complex than most observers think. To move in the purposeful, measured, controlled way of the discipline takes total concentration, muscle coordination, and balance. I've fallen flat on my face when my thoughts moseyed away from the exercise more times than I like to admit.

Disappointed, I staked out a spot in the last row. I really, really wanted to punch and bite and scream and kick.

From my corner, I saw the instructor's back. Tyler teaches evening sessions so he can handle the business end of the studio during daytime hours. He hires other black belts for those classes. This woman was small and slender, and if I weren't at a *dojo*, I might have thought of her as delicate and vulnerable. Here, I knew the white cotton *gi* hid the kind of power I needed to keep sane and continue to live day after day. Weakness is unthinkable.

The *sensei* turned. "We'll start with the usual Push the Mountain."

My stomach crashed to my toenails. I'd never given much credence to the existence of devils, demons, and other such tormentors, but at that moment something told me I was on my way to becoming a believer; they were having a field day with me.

Detective Tsu was teaching the class.

If my presence surprised her as much as hers did me, she didn't show it on her exquisite Asian face. She didn't acknowledge me but instead went right into the lesson.

As a measure of how far I'd come the last few years, I was able to focus and forget the detective's presence until everyone bowed at the end of the session.

Since I didn't want her to think she scared the stuffing out of me or that I had anything to hide, I approached her as the room emptied of other students.

"Good morning. I'm surprised to see you here."

Detective Tsu arched a brow. "I've taught this class for three years."

"Well, I usually come at night, but now that I don't have much to keep me busy . . ." I shrugged. "I'd rather keep my evenings free."

"Ah . . . an active social life."

Whenever I'm nervous I laugh, so I laughed. Once I settled down to chortles, I said, "Yeah, right. I have a standing date with two guys every night."

Her eyes opened wide in obvious shock.

Aha! I'd caught her off guard. "One's a really, really furry blond who likes to cuddle after cozy Eukanuba dinners, and the other's my dad."

"Okay." The detective headed for the showers. "I'm glad we got that straight."

The woman made me antsy. Not only could she ruin my life if she bungled the investigation into Marge's murder, but she also lacked a vital personal component—she had no sense of humor. Fine. I'd try a different, more direct tack.

I followed her into the locker room. "Any news?"

"What kind of news would you like, Ms. Farrell?"

I stopped pulling pins from my hair. "Are you kidding me? You practically accused me of killing my mentor the last time we spoke, and now you want to know what kind of news I want?"

The cop shrugged, but her gaze said there was nothing blasé about her. She had the upper hand.

"Fine. You want me to put it in so many words? Well, I'm no coward." Oh, sure. And if I say it enough times I might someday believe it too. "Do you have the results of Marge's autopsy? Have you learned anything new?"

My heart beat so hard I could hardly breathe.

Detective Tsu let me sweat—I really had to be more careful what I wished for. This wasn't the kind of sweating I'd look forward to when I came to the *dojo*. She turned toward the bank of lockers and clicked in a combination. She then took out a classy leather duffel bag and a soft cream and gold cosmetics case. Without another look my way, she went to the nearest shower, set her bags on the bench at its side, and rummaged through her belongings.

I felt like dumping her fancy stuff on the floor so she could find what she wanted and then answer my questions. But like a good little Tai Chi student, I kept my cool.

Finally, with a thick ivory towel hung from the hook on the wall and coordinated French-perfume toiletries in hand, Detective Tsu walked into the shower.

That was rude. "I did ask you a question, and in view of my position, I don't think I'm out of line. The least you could do is—"

"The least I can do," she said, curtain in hand, "is to remember I'm a professional. I can't discuss an ongoing investigation, and I'm sure you've watched enough TV to know that. Even scriptwriters don't have a detective share data with—"

"The prime suspect." Now I knew I had the top of their list all to myself. "Don't let me keep you. Take your shower. We wouldn't want even a whiff of impropriety to hang around you."

Again, her eyes widened, and it was all I could do to keep from smacking my forehead. How could I let this ice princess rattle me like that? I had to get a grip if I was to keep myself out of jail.

I snagged my army surplus duffel bag and left before I pulled another dumb stunt. Like a homing pigeon, I shot straight for my car.

I almost made it too. Tyler blocked the *dojo* door.

"You can't get behind the wheel right now. We have to talk."

Sometimes being a grown-up is a royal pain. "You're right. I'm too mad to handle a lethal weapon."

I collapsed into the very American overstuffed couch in Tyler's office. He loves all things Asian, as the shelf of fabulous carvings and the framed watercolors on the room's walls shows. But the *sensei* also loves his creature comforts—he draws the line at sitting with clients on a mat-covered floor.

He took the corner opposite me. "I won't ask what got you like this. So why don't you explain that murder one thing."

"It's all the same." A familiar sensation clawed to life in the pit of my stomach. "Why didn't you tell me you had a hotshot cop teaching lessons?"

"Why didn't you ask?"

"Okay. You want me to be reasonable, but you know? I'm way past that. Did you read yesterday's paper?"

He waved toward his desk. "It's somewhere in here. I didn't get a chance to look at it. Mei-Li fussed all day long, and Sarah got called in to an emergency surgery."

Tyler's five-month-old daughter is a sweetie, but teething isn't going well.

"Sorry. As bad as it must have been, it doesn't come close to the grim content in my last two days."

"So? When are you going to tell me? I know whatever's got hold of you is bad. I've watched you long enough now to know when something's exploded on you."

"That's putting it mildly." I fought the nausea, squared my shoulders, pressed the palms of my hands against my knees. I took a couple of even breaths. "Someone killed Marge on Wednesday. And I was the one who found her."

The first curse I'd ever heard him utter ripped from Tyler's mouth. His eyes turned cold, scary, and the smooth brown skin on his cheeks tightened.

"Why didn't you call me?" His voice was soft, yet I knew my failure to turn to him bothered him, maybe even hurt.

My exasperated sigh blew loose hair from my forehead. "Because I didn't have time to even think. As if that wasn't bad enough, Marge left me everything—all that money, the business, even that new cedar, glass, and steel house of hers."

"And Lila thinks you did it."

"I guess you know her pretty well."

"I do, but it's a standard thing to suspect whoever benefits most from the murder." He fiddled with the exercise ball he kept at hand. "It's also common for them to look at the husband in these cases. I bet Lila's giving Steve Norwalk a hard time too."

I studied the cranes in the watercolor over his head. "Last I heard, he was out of town since Wednesday at a teacher's seminar or something. That's why he missed the Gerrity sale. That sounds to me like a pretty good alibi."

Tyler stood, and out the corner of my eye, I noticed his frown. "I don't know why you're so upset. It's not a matter of alibis or anything. You didn't hurt Marge, and soon enough Lila's going to realize it. So chill."

I stood and paced from one end of the room to the other. "You don't understand. It's not just that. But I'll tell you, your friend, Detective Lila Tsu? She's a pretty scary character."

Tyler smiled and crossed his arms.

I ignored his reaction. "On top of everything else, the mansion's off-limits. It's the scene of a crime, and the police have it cordoned off. It can't be sold, so Noreen Daventry can't buy it. Since she can't buy it, she can't hire me to redesign it. Since she can't hire me—"

"I get the picture. But come on. I'm sure you can get a job or two if you really try. It might not be as flashy as that big old place, but fixing up a basement family room will pay some bills."

"The Stokers did hire me to do their living and dining rooms." Why did I keep forgetting the couple who'd be my first real customers? "I should call them and take a look at the space."

When Tyler didn't respond, I shot him a glance. Uh-oh. I knew that look. It was the one that announced outgoing questions.

"What's the real problem, Haley?" he asked. "Is this too close to what happened four years ago?"

My hard-won progress vanished. I again felt my attacker's strength. I don't think I screamed, but I might have, because a sharp sound rang out. All I knew was pain and fear.

My ears buzzed. I shivered. I wrapped my arms around me, but they couldn't protect me. A gentle force at my back moved me forward. Like a robot, I went. I was told to sit. I did.

Desperation almost smothered me, but its return somehow made me react. From somewhere deep inside, I dredged up a spark of anger. That I could handle, so I clung to the flicker. I could beat the confusion, pain, and fear if I stoked the flicker into a full-blown furnace blaze.

I opened my eyes. At first, the red walls made me think real flames surrounded me. Then slowly I remembered where I was. The *dojo* . . . Tyler . . .

"She was helpless!" My words came out raw; my throat felt even more so. "He hit her from behind."

I cried. Big, gulping, convulsive sobs tore through me. Stinging tears poured down my cheeks. I couldn't stand to think that the woman who'd stood by me and helped me find footing—find myself—after I went through living hell had now been subjected to the ultimate victimization.

After a while I brought my misery under control. I wiped my cheeks with the backs of my hands, shoved my hair out of my face. Again I clung to the rage, and with its help I stood.

I looked at Tyler. His expression showed concern. "I'm okay," I said. "As okay as I can be, considering the circumstances."

He didn't believe me.

My wry grimace changed nothing. But I was going to be okay. I didn't know when or how, but I had been down this road before.

I've learned a lot. Thanks to Tyler, my body can withstand a lot more now than before I met him, but only if I use my head. I had to focus on what mattered.

The top to my *gi* had become twisted somewhere along the line, and I straightened it. I usually showered and changed after class, but no way was I going to risk another face-to-face with Detective Tsu. Anger kicked in again.

Good. That would help me focus. "Tell you what, *sensei*. I'm not going to let your fellow instructor shut me up in jail. And I'm not going to let her build such a crummy case that whoever killed Marge gets away with it."

"Really?"

Tyler's mild tone spurred me. "Yeah, really. Last time, the cops and the court messed up big time, and that creep got off with just a slap on his hand. This time, I'm going to make sure justice happens."

"And how are you going to do it?"

That tripped me up for half a heartbeat. "I'm not a cop, but I can pester them until they do their job. Then I can bug the prosecutor until his case is airtight. The jury and the jail can do the rest."

"Hmm . . . so you're going to become a one-woman ultimate judge."

"Someone has to. Look at what happened to me."

"What makes you think that ultimate judge isn't already on the job and that he doesn't do it better than you ever could?"

"Don't start with all that God stuff again, Tyler. I know where you and Dad stand, but until you've crawled through the pit I got shoved in, don't tell me how just and good and . . . and . . . whatever else you say God is."

He lowered his head, and I could tell he was praying. It made me uncomfortable, but I couldn't ask him to stop when I didn't want him to ask me to start.

I thought I heard a whispered amen.

"Let me know when you let him catch you in those warm, strong, loving arms of his again," he said.

My breath caught. I didn't have words to reject his. Something about them made me sad. As if I wasn't already sad enough.

I grabbed my duffel bag and opened the office door.

"God bless you, Haley."

I once treasured those words so freely given by my devout Christian parents and friends. But after God left me at the mercy of a monster, I no longer give them much weight.

"Don't hold your breath." I closed the door, hurried through the lobby, and burst into the drizzly, gray day. I didn't want to meet Detective Tsu again, nor even the nice women I'd met before class. I was too . . . too . . . I didn't have the words to express all I felt. One feeling I could identify.

I couldn't remember ever feeling this alone.

I drove away.

5

For the last six months, Saturday mornings meant a crowded store with fussy furniture buyers. They do no more. Now Saturday's about to become a worse form of torture. I have to cross the parking lot between the manse and the church and preside over the missionary society. I know nothing about their business, even though I know the members pretty well.

After my close encounter with Tyler's faith the day before, I dreaded today's meeting more than I otherwise would have. If possible.

For a nanosecond I wished I could beg off and go sell bilious couches to people with too much money and too little taste. But then an especially unfortunate episode with a well-heeled woman who loved all things orange and plum came to mind.

"That's a quick cure," I told Midas. I doubted Penny Harham would approve of my dog's presence at the meeting, but the other ladies had asked me to bring him along. The Golden One is a favorite with Dad's flock.

"Well, it's about time you got here," Penny groused the moment I opened the door to Room A. "Your tardiness is more proof of your lack of interest in the society's business."

Ina Appleton smacked a white china mug of coffee in front of the postal clerk, but in an even, pleasant voice she said, "It's exactly nine oh two, Penny. The society's meetings have never started less than fifteen minutes late. Please give our new president the benefit of the doubt."

Penny pursed her lips. "And whose fault are the late starts, Mrs. Hospitality Chair in Perpetuity? I've never seen coffee perk as slow as when you make it."

"The urn's not as young as it used to be," Ina replied. Her tight smile showed what it cost to keep the peace. "Just like the rest of us."

Penny stiffened. "Speak for yourself. There are those of us who pride ourselves on our young-at-heart spirits."

"And it's for the well-being of our spirits," Gussie said, "that we meet to consider the needs of the missionaries we support."

Wow. Impressive. Those sweetly voiced, gentle words had sure packed a punch. Penny's leather-tanned cheeks turned the color of bricks.

A rousing cheer rose from the far end of the table. "Go get 'em, Gussie girl!"

Bella Cahill is one of the most outspoken people I've ever met. She's also a true original, and she proves it every chance she gets. Four months ago she celebrated her seventieth birthday. That day she showed up in church with her hair cut into a choppy Hollywood style and dyed magenta. In spite of repeated efforts to return it to its initial glory, the moppy mess has now faded to an odd shade of Pepto-Bismol pink.

"How's it going, Haley?" she asked.

"I'm okay."

She ogled my outfit. "Like your shorts. I think I'll go get me a pair just like 'em when we're done here."

I looked from my bike shorts to the pudgy woman. As beautiful as Bella had once been, and we all knew she'd graced the cover of every fashion magazine in her day, the decades had melted the lean and elegant lines to Michelin-man rolls. But if Bella wanted her Rubenesque thighs stuffed into bike shorts, more power to her. In the Seattle area, even senior citizens can look . . . unique and nobody will look twice.

"Bella Cahill," Penny chided. "Act your age."

Well, almost nobody.

"Hey!" the offended party yelped. "Didn't you just say you were young at heart? Well? How young is that?"

Gussie gave a ladylike *ahem.* "Penny, I'm sure that Bella will find appropriate shorts. Besides, that's not the reason we're here. The Randalls' efforts are bearing wonderful fruit. The school has grown faster than they thought it would, and now they need to add an eighth grade. What would be the best way to fund textbooks and other supplies?"

My admiration for Gussie, always great, was now eclipsed by my gratitude. I had no clue how to handle the missionary society, but she'd calmly and sweetly taken the reins and run with it. All I had to do was offer an occasional uh-huh and scratch Midas's head each time he begged, which was often.

I let the murmur of women's voices lull me into a thoughtful state. Because of the way I wound up with my unexpected inheritance, I don't want it. But I can't just refuse it. True, I don't have to use it, but then, what's the point of letting it all go to waste? Especially when people like the Randalls can use it to help little kids in terrible need. I can see why Mom had devoted so much time to the missionary society.

All of a sudden, I noticed the shrieking silence. Every eye skewered me. Penny in particular wore an I-had-canary-for-breakfast smile.

It sure looked like I, on the other hand, had trouble for my midmorning snack. When no one spoke, I turned to Gussie. "What? What'd I do?"

Penny snorted.

Gussie blushed.

Bella whistled. "You hit the jackpot!"

"Huh?"

Gussie tsk-tsked. "Oh, Bella. That's a terrible thing to say. Marge is dead, and you know how much Haley loved her."

So much for my lull. The grief was back in spades.

"True," Bella said, unrepentant. "But that love never really croaks, ya know? Money's just for stuff this side of heaven. Think of all she can do with all that dough. It's not as if Marge was snuffed and no one'll be the wiser to her life. Haley loved—loves—her, and she can even come up with memorials or something like that." Bella beamed bright blue eyes on me. "So what're you gonna do with all the bucks?"

Talk about being put on the spot. "I haven't given it a thought. I just want to help the police find the killer."

If my ears didn't deceive me, Penny muttered, "A likely story."

Bella's cheeks turned rosy. "Woo-hoo! Can I help? I'd be real good at it too. I've got every last episode of *Murder, She Wrote* on tape and a copy of every single book on my bookshelf. I've even got Angela Lansbury's autograph on a couple of 'em."

"Bella, that's just a TV show. I'm not going to do anything like that. I just meant that I'm cooperating with the police investigation. That's all."

Bella's smile went south. "Oh. Well, it was a good idea."

"Why don't we close in prayer?" Gussie asked, her smile full of sympathy for me. "I'll take the lead today, ladies."

I hadn't foreseen this, and if Tyler's prayers had made me uncomfortable, Gussie's sincere thanks and praise made me feel like the worst kind of heel. How had I let a cotton-fluff bully rope me into this goofy presidency?

With the silk and satin lasso of her kindness and friendship is how. Gussie is awesome.

When she'd finished, Gussie rolled her wheelchair to my side. "Why don't you and your dad come over for supper tonight? That way you can look at the rooms and take measurements, and we can talk colors and furniture."

"Sounds good. What time would you like us?"

"Hey!" Bella cried. "I thought I was coming for dinner."

Gussie reached out and patted her friend's plump hand. "Of course you are. I just figured the more the merrier."

"All right," Bella said, her million-dollar smile as potent as ever. "Maybe we can talk Haley into some sleuthing while we're at it."

"We'll do no such thing," Gussie countered. "It's a better idea if we join in prayer and ask the Lord to watch over everyone involved."

Another trap I hadn't foreseen.

Oh well. I was committed now, and I really did need the job. I'd just have to find a way to escape the prayer stuff.

Later that afternoon as I packed my paint chips, my tape measure, and my camera, Midas went into a barking frenzy. I went downstairs, even though I hadn't heard the doorbell over his greeting. He was better than a burglar alarm. Unfortunately, he was a lousy guard dog. All he wanted was to play with the new arrival.

Through the front window, I saw the police cruiser in the driveway. No one sat inside today, so whoever drove it was already at the door.

"Detective Tsu," I said a moment later. "You mean you still have more questions?"

"Of course, but that's not why I'm here. Yesterday at the *dojo* you asked if I had any news. I received the autopsy report late last night, and it will be made public today. I've come as a courtesy to let you know the results."

"Thank goodness! For a while there, I was afraid you guys were going to pin the crime on me just because I somehow touched the rock that killed Marge. My hand probably landed on it when I fainted."

She narrowed her eyes. "I'm afraid that's not the case, Ms. Farrell. The autopsy came back with no additional cause for Mrs. Norwalk's death. She died from the blow to the back of her head. And the rock had bits of brain material on it."

My gag reflex kicked in. I fisted my hands at my sides. I counted my breaths . . . long, measured, controlled. "I suppose your visit also means they found no other fingerprints on the stone."

She gave me a slow nod.

A chill ran through me. "You have considered the possibility of a gloved killer, haven't you?"

The cop shrugged.

"Look, Ms. Tsu, do you really think I'd be so stupid as to draw attention to Marge's body if I'd killed her? Do you think I'd have stayed around after I'd done it?"

"I've spent ten years on the force, Ms. Farrell. I've learned that anything's possible, and even more so, likely."

"Well, I didn't kill Marge. And you'd better do a better job of finding the person who did, because I'm not going to sit around and let you hang it on me."

There. I'd told her what I'd said to Tyler the day before. Why didn't I feel any better?

Maybe Ms. Tsu's non-response had something to do with it.

Midas pranced up to the detective and slurped her arm with a sloppy, doggy kiss. Benedict Arnold had nothing on my dog.

A smile—a real one—brightened the cop's face. She really is a beautiful woman, and evidently, a dog lover too. Too bad she's such a lousy detective. A better one would know I couldn't have hurt Marge, or anyone else, for that matter.

"You're a big, beautiful boy, aren't you?" Ms. Tsu said.

Midas's bliss knew no bounds when she scratched the sweet spot behind his left ear. His tail thwacked the door frame in a jackhammer beat.

"How old is he?"

"He turned four in March."

Ms. Tsu murmured more sweet nothings in my turncoat dog's ear. "Mine died last November. I still miss her."

"You had a golden?"

The detective arched a brow. "You know, Ms. Farrell, cops are people too."

I blushed hot and hard.

She went on. "My job's not easy, and I don't get many thanks. Just remember, I didn't have to come and tell you anything. I just did what I would have wanted had I been in your shoes."

I sighed. "There's no excuse for my rudeness. I'm sorry. The last two days have been tough. I appreciate your consideration, even though I can assure you you're on the wrong track. I didn't kill Marge Norwalk, and I'm afraid you're wasting precious time on me while evidence . . . clues . . . whatever gets damaged."

"I'm very good at what I do," she countered.

I thought back to yesterday's Tai Chi lesson. The woman had exceptional concentration, and her controlled movements revealed a great deal of strength.

I forced a smile. "No doubt you are. Was there anything else?"

"You do realize you can't leave town without police approval, don't you?"

"I hadn't given it a thought. First, I have no plans to go anywhere, and second, I have no reason to think that way."

"We shall see, Ms. Farrell. We shall see."

As she went toward the patrol car, I called out, "I'll bet you're one of Tyler's teacher's-pet black belts."

She turned, and her eyes zeroed in on mine. Then she laughed. "I could get to like you. And I think Tyler meant it as a warning when he told me that after yesterday's class. He knows I'd have a hard time arresting a potential friend. Let's hope his faith in you isn't misplaced."

My jaw nearly hit the floor.

There was no reading this woman. But I didn't need a novel to learn how much trouble I was in. I had to talk to Tyler about Detective Tsu.

I savored another bit of dinner. "Gussie, the turkey tenderloins are incredible. You're the best cook I know."

"That's why I worm an invitation out of her every chance I get," Bella said, her plate piled high with turkey, broccoli and carrot salad, and rice pilaf. "It's a blessing she's also the most generous person I know."

Tom gave his wife a tender look. "I'm the luckiest man around."

Gussie looked down. "Thanks. You're too flattering."

To help the woman who'd bailed me out that morning, I said, "Tell me what exactly you and Tom want to change in these two rooms. I've rarely seen a home as nice or as charming as yours."

"It is nice," Gussie answered, "but after all these years, the upholstery shows a lot of wear, and I'm pretty tired of the same things day in and day out. I'd love to have something new and fresh to look forward to every morning."

Uninvited, the words of one of my mother's favorite hymns

trickled through my mind. It spoke about God's mercies and how they were new every morning. I sighed. It'd been a long time since I'd last felt those mercies. Marge's murder didn't seem to fit in with them either.

Determined to stay focused, I looked around the room and asked, "Does this layout work with your wheelchair?"

"The dining room's fine," Gussie answered. "But the living room feels like a minefield. I don't think lining the furniture up against the walls was the answer."

I groaned. "That's my number one pet peeve."

"Hey, I have the solution to that problem," Bella said. "The best way to watch my new large-screen TV is in bed, so I went down to the store and bought myself a couple of mattresses. I had a friend nail together a platform in the middle of the room so we could plunk the mattresses on it, and then I bought some funky faux-fur stuff to cover the whole thing. Now I have perfect living room furniture. Everyone can lie down and still have the best seat in the house."

The idea made my teeth hurt.

Dad scratched his chin and gave a thoughtful, "Hmm . . ." He then added, "It sounds quite sybaritic, Bella. Somewhat along the Greco-Roman Empire line."

"Nope, Pastor Hale. I bought the mattresses new. I'm sure they've nothing to do with parasites. I know all about parasites. My vet told me all about them when Bali H'ai had that urping problem. It turned out to be hairballs."

Every time Bella mentioned her noxious long-haired cat, I fought my laughter. Anyone who asked about the name got the standard answer. *"Ever see South Pacific? Bali H'ai's exotic, isn't it? Well, so's she."*

Since I couldn't stand the thought of sitting in on Dad's lecture on Sybaris, the Greeks, the Romans, the fall of the various empires, and Bella's beast, I rooted through my backpack purse until I felt the camera.

"I'm going to take pictures so I know what we have to work with," I told Gussie. "That way I won't have to rely on my memory or bug you every time I want to check on something."

Gussie waved me toward the living room. "Do you mind if I follow? I've never had an interior designer do a room for me, and I'm curious to see how you do what you do. I'm a little excited too."

Glad for the chance to entertain Gussie, I grabbed the wheelchair handles and guided her toward the living room. "I'd never do a thing without your input. A good designer only interprets what the client likes and wants."

"Oh, we're going to have so much fun!"

Behind us, a chair scraped the floor. "Hey, wait for me!" Bella cried. "I want in on the fun too. Besides, I brought Haley a present."

I paused. "A present?"

Bella nodded her shaggy pink head. "Wait'll you get a load of this. It's the best on the market."

Uh-oh.

"See?" Bella asked, a small silver canister in her hand. "After Penny told us a bunch of stupid lies about you, the cops, and the murder, I got to thinking that you could find yourself in a barrel of trouble. I had to make sure you could protect yourself against the killer."

Gussie pressed the control button for the wheelchair motor and rolled to Bella's side. "That was a nice gesture, Bella, whatever that is. But Haley can take excellent care of herself. She's a martial arts expert."

"Really?" Bella's cup of excitement did indeed runneth over. "Can you show me how to break a stack of bricks with one chop?"

"Um . . . it takes a lot of practice to do something like that, and I'm not a teacher."

Bella considered my words. She shrugged. "Eh. True enough. How about you show me how to kick some jerk in the chin, then? I'm an old lady, and I don't want a purse snatcher to get away with my stuff."

Somehow, the image of roly-poly Bella kickboxing failed to gel. How do I get myself into this kind of mess all the time? "That's another thing you'd be better off learning from a real teacher. I'll give you the number for Tyler Colby's *dojo*, and he can teach you any martial arts move you want to learn."

"Dough-joe, dough-joe! Is that cool or what?"

I'd never seen Bella so animated. I had a funny feeling she'd swap bike shorts for a *gi* before too long.

"Anyway," she said after a few more rounds of the mangled chant, "here's your super-duper, giant-sized, extra-strength can of mace. The boy behind the counter said it was the best kind. He even showed me how to use it."

Gussie looked at me just as I looked at her. Bella with a can of mace was scary.

I held out a hand. "I'll take it, Bella. And thank you for thinking of me."

"You're welcome, honey. But you gotta let me help when you go sniff out the killer."

"I already said I'm not doing anything like that."

As if she hadn't heard me, and maybe she hadn't, since she was riveted by the can of mace, Bella added, "Here. Let me show you how easy this is."

"That's all right, I can read the instructions—"

"See the little thingy here? That's the trigger. But you have to be very careful. It's mega-sensitive."

At that moment a gray streak flew across the room. It gave an inhuman shriek before it landed at Bella's feet. Startled, she tottered and nearly trampled her maniacal cat.

"Bali H'ai, you naughty girl. Why'd you leave your little bag-house? I told you I'd give you liver treats if you waited for me in there."

The cat puffed up and nipped Bella's ankle.

I couldn't blame Bali H'ai. If Bella offered me liver in exchange for good behavior, I might decide to bite her too.

But that feline nibble had its consequences.

That mega-sensitive button on the canister?

It was sensitive, all right. Lucky for us, Bella either was given the wrong thing or had gotten confused. It wasn't mace she sprayed. She got us with pepper spray instead.

The burn of a red-hot steel rod ground into my eyes.

6

If you have to get hit with self-defense spray, then you're a whole lot better off if it's the pepper spray kind that gets you. Sure, you'll feel as if someone stuck you on a barbecue spit because they want to serve you up for Sunday dinner, but this effect lasts only about twenty minutes, and the worst that can happen is that you might rub your eyes and make them sting even more.

Mace, on the other hand, not only makes your eyes burn and slam shut but also makes you disoriented, restricts your breathing, causes uncontrolled coughing, and even brings on temporary blindness. All these spiffy results last about a half hour, sometimes more. And that "sometimes more" is the key. There's that controversy about those random arrest cases where the perp dies.

Mace is nasty, and I was forever indebted to the kid who sold Bella pepper spray rather than mace.

Which isn't to say that pepper spray isn't a bear of a beast to fight off. I'd taken the time to learn all about self-defense. Unfortunately, I did it too late to help myself four years ago. Nowadays, I have a can of each in my bag.

When Bali H'ai and Bella demonstrated how easy the canister was to use, I hit the ground like everyone else, eyes streaming, face burning.

"Don't rub your eyes," I cried. I sobbed and rubbed with all I had.

Oh, you'll rub, no matter how well you know you shouldn't.

"I can't help it," Bella wailed, rubbing with a vengeance.

I crawled toward relief. It was hard, since every couple of inches I had to stop and rub some more. I aimed for the kitchen sink to rinse my face, hands, and eyes. I hoped I'd find enough kitchen towels to soak and share with Bella's other victims. Bella too. I didn't want her to suffer.

I'm not sure how I made it to the sink. But I did, and I also opened the back door to air the house.

Moments later I handed out wet towels. "Here. Use them and head out. Be careful!"

The improvement didn't last once I was back in the living room, but I grabbed Gussie's wheelchair and, between swipes at my enraged eyes and gentle shoves to the chair, we reached the front door.

"Bella is something else," I muttered.

Gussie gave a teary chuckle. "She always has been. That's why she's such fun to have around."

"This is fun?"

"No, of course not." Gussie's wet towel muffled her voice. "Sometimes her fun goes wild. Today's one of those times."

"I'll say." The cool evening air did wonders for my stinging cheeks. "Can you imagine her 'helping' the cops?"

"It boggles the mind, doesn't it?"

I patted Gussie's shoulder. "And then some."

Now that I could see again, I noticed the others had come around to the front garden. They too were on the way to recovery. "If you don't mind, I'm going to open the windows. We need to air the house if you want to sleep tonight."

Gussie smiled in spite of her red nose and swollen eyes. "Go ahead. I'm fine. Besides, everyone needs a little shake-up now and then."

"A little shake-up . . ." I shook my head, not sure I needed any more shake-up, with all that had happened in the last few days. I ran from room to room and opened the many windows.

A short while later, after Bella's efforts on my behalf had amused the neighbors, Dad and I went home. The evening was classic Pacific Northwest: cool, breezy, enjoyable. Wilmont being as small as Seattle is huge, we'd walked to the Stoker home, and now I was glad. The exercise did wonders to soothe my ruffled nerves, especially after the pepper-spray attack.

"Oh, for goodness' sake," Dad grumbled as we approached the driveway to the manse. "Why can't that girl understand? How many times do I have to tell her she shouldn't drop the newspaper in the lawn because most of the time it's wet in our part of the world and leftover rain ruins newspapers?"

Dad's battle of wills with the determined teen, a newer member of his church's youth group, made me smile. In my opinion, the odds in this war are on the girl. Something about the twinkle in her eye and the dry newspaper on our back step clued me in.

Dad too, even though he'll never admit it. He loves to tease Sandy Appleton as much as she loves to tease him. The size of her tip on collection day at the end of every month proves it.

"I'll get it, Dad. Just go on in."

He grinned. "Thanks. I'll go around back."

I laughed. He'll never say a word about the dry paper in the recycling bin tomorrow morning, and neither will I. It was a nutty deal, but Sandy has made a terrific turnaround since she's taken up the paper route. Her school's truancy officer reports that she hasn't missed a single day of class, and her grandmother Ina, a member of the missionary society, says the rough crowd hasn't been around for a while.

Dad's visits to Ina and Sandy, apple muffins in hand, have become weekly events. So has Sandy's presence in church on Sundays.

I don't get it, but if Sandy buys the God deal, what can I say?

I bent and gathered the soggy wad of paper and, without meaning to, noticed the headlines. Marge's murder led the day's news. A crime of that magnitude didn't often happen in Wilmont. Then a line from the article jumped out at me—"Because such a vast fortune is involved, the police have a strong suspect, and the lead investigator assures this reporter that an arrest is imminent."

The pepper spray had nothing on this for inciting an extreme physical response. Every part of me froze. Except for my knees. They seemed to melt. It took all my energy to walk to the porch. I'd barely reached it when the front door opened and Dad came out, newspaper in hand.

"Honey . . . ?"

I nodded, unable to speak.

Dad's whispered prayer and his comforting arm reached me at the same time. The arm I could accept; the prayer . . . well, let's just say I wanted no part of a God who had left me high and dry again.

We walked into the cozy living room, and as I sat in Mom's rocker, the phone rang. Dad picked it up. After a greeting and a couple of additional words, he held it out. "Sounds official."

I winced but took it anyway. "Hello?"

"Good evening, Ms. Farrell. It's Sam Harris."

"Yes?"

"Um . . . it's come to my notice that you might be in some trouble here."

When I didn't respond, he ummed and aahed some more. Then he cleared his throat. "What I mean to say is . . . well, you're going to need legal representation, and since I'm already the attorney of record for Mrs. Norwalk's affairs, it would make things easier if you retained me for the criminal matter."

The gall of the man stunned me silent.

"You do see the advantage, don't you?"

"Yeah. To you. But I don't need a lawyer. I haven't done a thing, and the cops are just slow finding the killer. I'll thank you to leave me alone—"

"Ms. Farrell, you don't understand how serious your situation is. You're the only person with motive, means, and opportunity. Those three things are what law enforcement considers crucial for zeroing on their man . . . er . . . woman, in this case."

"The conversation's over, Mr. Harris. Don't call me again. If I need you for Marge's business, I'll call you."

In my twenty-five years, I'd never hung up on anyone. I hadn't thought I could be that rude. But it felt good—great, actually. The sleazy shyster and the cheating builder would make a great team. I wonder if Harris represented Dutch in his lawsuit.

"I gather it wasn't the police," Dad said, TV clicker in hand. It was almost time for the ten o'clock news, and he never misses the program. He says he has to check before bedtime to see what the Lord wants him to pray about.

"You got that right. It was Marge's weasel lawyer." I blew at some strands of hair that had fallen over my eyes. "Can you believe he offered to represent me?"

"I thought he already represented Marge's estate. Doesn't that sort of cover representing you too?"

"Oh, he didn't call about the will or the estate, Dad. He figures I need a criminal lawyer."

My father closed his gray eyes. "I guess he read the paper."

"Must have. Either that or he's been chatting up his pals at the cop shop again."

I tried to keep my tone light, but my turkey tenderloin dinner was now ready to rumble. What was Detective Tsu doing if the best she could come up with was to pin this thing on me?

"Don't worry, Dad. I'll figure it out. The cops can't be so dumb as to think I killed Marge. Sooner or later they'll find the killer."

For the first time I could remember, Dad didn't turn on his newscast. He put the clicker down on the coffee table, then gathered up his Bible and headed for the stairs.

At the bottom step he turned and said, "Haley, I know the Father will see you through this, but I suspect that before that happens, things will get much worse. You might want to find yourself an advocate. I'd rather you reach out to the Lord, but you should hire a lawyer too. A different one, since you dislike this man so much."

I didn't have a decent answer, so I only said, "Good night."

When his bedroom door closed, I headed for the kitchen. Midas's nails clicked on the hardwood floor as he followed. The doggy cookie I tossed him didn't get the chance to hit the floor.

I smiled. At least one person didn't care what the cops thought. True, he had four paws and thick golden fur, but as far as Midas was concerned, he was just as human as the next guy . . . dog . . . whatever.

After a cup of chamomile tea, my stomach felt better, but I didn't. The newspaper article made everything too real. I was halfway through my fifth read when the phone rang.

"Haley?"

"Gussie! I'm surprised you're still awake."

"Tom brought in the evening paper, and after I read that article, I couldn't relax. How are you doing?"

"Just peachy dandy."

"I figured." Gussie's sigh felt almost as comforting as the gentle touch of her hand. "What are you going to do?"

"Aside from not hiring Marge's crummy lawyer, who just called to make me a generous offer I definitely could, and did, refuse? I don't know. I'll tell you this though. I'm not going to jail for something I didn't do."

"Of course not. Why would you?"

"Because the cops can't see what's before their noses."

"What do you see before your nose?"

"One of three people did it."

She gasped. "Who . . . who do you think killed Marge?"

"Well, according to TV shows and newspaper stories, conventional wisdom says the spouse did it. I know Steve wasn't in town, but maybe he was and only pretended to be gone. You know, building himself an alibi."

"That's . . . possible." Gussie didn't sound so sure.

I tore off a narrow strip of newsprint and balled it up. "There's always the business connection."

"Ozzie?" The shock in Gussie's voice was almost funny.

Before I could explain myself, she added, "Are you sure about that? From all I've seen, Ozzie is the most loyal employee a person could want."

"Maybe they disagreed on an auction or an item. Who knows? Maybe . . . oh, I don't know. I just know I didn't do it, and Steve and Ozzie are the two other people closest to Marge. Unless some deranged serial killer stopped by at the sale. That's my third and favorite choice, of course."

"You know that's not likely."

"That's why I'm sure it must have been Ozzie or Steve."

"Then why do the police seem so sure you did it? I mean, aside from the inheritance, but then, anyone who knows you knows that's got nothing to do with anything."

My point exactly. "Beats me, but the article makes it clear they're not looking at anyone else. They should, and if they don't start pretty soon, then I'm going to make sure they do."

"What are you going to do?"

I made a face. "Maybe Bella does have a point."

"Haley! You wouldn't—"

"Wait, Gussie. Hear me out." I hadn't given it much thought, but somewhere in the back of my mind, an idea was taking shape, one, I had to admit, that Bella had planted. "I'm going to think about this some more and then maybe ask a couple of questions. I'm sure I'll come up with something to tell the cops."

"Oh, Haley. This sounds like trouble. Bella's never too far from the edge of disaster, you know. You don't want to follow her."

"Don't worry. I won't do anything crazy. And I won't spray mace on anyone either."

"Is that supposed to reassure me?"

"I guess not, but I can't sit here and wait until they show up with a pair of steel bracelets. You know I only wear silver."

Gussie gave a halfhearted chuckle. "Just be careful. Someone hated Marge enough to kill her. I wouldn't want you to upset that someone and get hurt. I . . . I love you, honey."

"Thanks." Gussie was one of the nicest people I knew, and I was glad she'd called. "Thanks for checking on me too. You didn't have to, but I'm glad we talked. You helped me clear my thoughts, and I now have a better idea what to do next."

"That really sets my mind at ease." Gussie's sarcasm wasn't wasted, but I wasn't about to back down. I was the one in danger of a change of address.

Gussie added, "I don't like the idea of you taking such risks, but I guess I'm going to have to be happy with it, right?"

"That's right. Now, you'd better run, run, run to bed before Tom takes my Starbucks away. Real punishment, you know."

This chuckle had more oomph. "Good night, Haley. And let me know what you find out. I am concerned about you."

"I know, but you shouldn't be. Now, get a good rest, and I'll talk to you again soon."

I hung up and stared at the phone. Maybe Bella did have the right idea. To a certain extent, that is. I wasn't about to turn into Angela Lansbury, nor was I going to start dressing out of L. L. Bean, but I could check out those two men. If nothing else, I had a couple of questions for Steve.

Tomorrow looked like a good day for answers.

Okay. So why did I ever think I could pull this off?

I'd driven past Marge's house about seventeen times already, and nothing came to me. I had no idea how to approach my mentor's widower.

Especially since he had company, company that was in no apparent hurry to leave.

A silver Jaguar sat in the driveway next to the Norwalks' Mercedes. For work, Marge had relied on a box truck; it could handle the tallest highboy or armoire. For herself, she'd used the VW Bug. She only used the Mercedes when she met new customers or when she and Steve went out together. The rest of the time, Steve used the posh vehicle. His drive to and from the school where he taught algebra and geometry was less than a five-mile round trip.

"Well, I'm not going to learn anything while I waste gas, am I?"

I pulled into a strip mall about a half mile away from the entrance to the enclave of mansions. That's what I called them. Most residents preferred the euphemism "luxury home."

They were luxurious, all right. I'd love to land a contract to do one or two. That'd set me up for years to come. But they'd still be mansions, no matter what.

At the moment, though, the only one I cared about was the cedar, glass, and steel one at the end of the cul-de-sac. I didn't bother to lock my Honda. It looked ridiculously humble among the Saabs, BMWs, Mercedes, and Volvos in the parking lot.

I hurried toward the Norwalk home. But by the time I reached the lush rhododendrons at the end of the long driveway, I still had nothing but the need to know who'd killed Marge. I'd take any idea right about now, no matter how crazy, even something Bella cooked up.

Oh, don't be such a wimp! Thus bolstered, I approached the front door. As I aimed for the bell, music wafted from the backyard.

Strange. You'd figure a widower of only days would be more likely to spend time in silent reflection remembering his late wife. But if I wasn't mistaken, Steve Norwalk had chosen the lush, sensual sound of Ravel's "Bolero" for this morning's tune.

I figured I'd better not make much noise. At the very least, I didn't know if I'd find the man weeping because the music had held some particular meaning for him and Marge. I wouldn't want to just burst in on him.

Then I heard a giggle. A feminine giggle. A flirty feminine giggle. That didn't sound like a lot of grieving going on.

I took my time and was pretty careful about where I crept. As I came to the end of the side walkway, I grinned. Up ahead sat the perfect cover. Because Marge's new home was such a chichi place, even the trash rated its own private abode. I'd laughed myself silly when she'd shown me the shed.

"Hey!" she'd cried. "I don't want garbage and recycling junk to mess up the curb appeal."

Now I was glad she'd had the foresight. If I pushed the cracked-open door a bit further, I could hide behind it and still see the backyard through the space between the hinges.

Which is what I did.

And nearly blew my excellent cover. The sight of Steve Norwalk and Noreen Daventry in bathing suits—if one could call the Band-Aids they wore on their buff bodies bathing suits—and wrapped around each other nearly made me puke.

How dare they! Poor Marge wasn't even in the ground yet, and here they were cavorting in her house, her pool. I glared at them.

They were way too close for new acquaintances. Had Marge known about the affair?

Maybe I wouldn't get to ask Steve any pointed questions today, but at least I'd learned something new. There was another suspect in the design of this crime, and her name was Noreen.

That brought up another question. Should I stay and see if I could hear anything that might incriminate them? Or should I head straight for Detective Tsu's office with my discovery?

As I pondered my dilemma, a strange squeak came from my left, right behind the gargantuan trash toter our fair hamlet provides its residents for their refuse.

I'm not crazy about scavengers. Give me dogs, cats, bunnies, even the occasional guinea pig, but real rodents? Reptiles? Vultures and buzzards? Uh-uh. I'll pass on those.

I scooted out as far as possible and still remain hidden behind the door. Of course, I tripped—on a huge beat-up running shoe, foot within.

To my credit, I didn't scream. But the inhuman squeal that rose from behind the trash can scared about ten years off my life. A pair of rats sped past me. Their humongous size horrified me, so I zigged when they zagged and brought my heel down on the grungy sneaker.

"What do you think you're doing?" Dutch snarled.

When my heart resumed beating, I said, "Ah . . . well . . . I wanted to pay my condolences . . . Yeah, that's it. I wanted to pay Steve Norwalk a condolence call."

Dutch gave me a look of pure disgust.

I didn't blame him. I wouldn't buy it either if I'd found the person who tried to feed it to me in a trash shed. So I figured it didn't really count as a lie. It was just a momentary diversion.

Another of those giggles rose over the notes of "Bolero."

Dutch looked over the door. I leaned to peer through my crack between the hinges. Thanks to Ravel, neither Noreen nor Steve seemed to have heard the rats. Their embrace had only grown steamier since I last checked.

"I'd never have pegged you for a peeping Tom," Dutch muttered. "Thomasina, actually."

"Those two are disgusting." I put more distance between us and waved poolward. "I can't believe they're—"

Crash!

No way the two on the lounge chair could've missed that. People in China heard the trash can fall. On me.

"Come on," Dutch ordered. "We have to get out of here before they call the cops and we're hauled in for trespassing."

He grabbed my arm and, before I scraped the wilted lettuce, coffee grounds, and soggy potato chips off my clothes, dragged me away. It wasn't an easy proposition, I'll give him that, since my sandals slid on repulsive green goo, but Dutch wasn't about to be thwarted.

"Oh, for crying out loud." With a final yank to my arm, he knocked me off balance and scooped me up in his arms.

Fear hitched in my throat. My heart pounded. He was too close. I was too vulnerable. Four years melted away.

He trotted off, and in spite of my efforts to escape, I noticed the wrapper stuck on his shoulder.

I laughed. It was a nervous laugh, shrill, full of strain, and on the verge of panic, but still a laugh. The label seemed appropriate. I might be garbed in produce past its prime, but Dutch bore a warning. The label on his shirt decreed him a Nutty Buddy.

Buddy? I didn't think so.

Nutty? Oh yeah.

7

"Put me down."

My demand gave him no leeway, and I know he heard it, since I made it mere millimeters from his ear.

It was a nice enough ear but, apparently, out of order.

He jogged down the drive, past the two pricey cars, and didn't pause when he reached the sidewalk. His stamina impressed me; his noncompliance didn't.

I had to get out of his clutches before a panic attack struck. I hadn't had one in about a year. Since he hadn't harmed me—yet—I held my breath for a couple of seconds, long enough for my heartbeat to resume a semiregular rhythm.

"Hey!" I smacked his shoulder, dislodging the Nutty Buddy wrapper. Pity. It suited him to a T. "What's wrong with you? Can't you hear? I said, put me down."

"Nothing's wrong with me, and my hearing's fine."

He didn't even sound out of breath. And I'm no teeny-mini woman. But I couldn't let his strength blind me to his insanity.

"I just have a healthy regard for freedom," he added. "We

have to get out of Dodge ASAP, and those funky sandals of yours look like they'd make lousy joggers."

"My Birkenstocks are excellent for everything."

"Not for staying ahead of the jailer."

"You should know."

That stopped him. I took advantage of his downgraded momentum to shove myself out of his grasp. I nearly landed on my rear.

Since he didn't answer, I stole a peek. Uh-oh. He wasn't happy.

"Just for the record," he said through gritted teeth, "I've never been arrested. Don't even get speeding tickets. None yet, and I'm thirty years old. That should tell you something."

"Yeah. You run faster than the law. And not by foot either."

"What's that supposed to mean?"

"That you got yourself a lawyer who kept you this side of trouble in that slippery slope mess you made."

As I indicted him, I heard Noreen, no longer out in the backyard.

Dutch looked back. "Come on. It'll be worse if she finds us here. Trust me on this."

My stomach did a nervous flutter. Trust was not one of my strong suits. Plus, his Tarzan swoop had brought back unbearable feelings. Loss of control didn't sit well with me.

"Fine. I'll go. On my own steam." My sandals slapped the concrete in a brisk beat.

Where did this sleazoid get off demanding answers, anyway? I was innocent. Well, innocent of everything except for maybe a wee bit of trespassing and eavesdropping. But what was his deal?

"So now that we're on our way to freedom, Dutch, how about you tell me what you were doing in Marge's trash shed?"

"I found you there, and I asked first. How about an answer?"

Thank goodness the strip mall was only about a block away. I'd had enough of Dutch. "I told you I came to pay my condolences—"

"Uh-huh. And the moon is made of marshmallows, and Mars of ketchup and beets."

"Gross!" I'd take a diversion any day. "Good thing you didn't go into cooking, even if you're a less than excellent builder—"

"You don't know a thing about me, so don't condemn me until you do. If you recall the stories you seem familiar with, I won that suit."

"That means nothing. Lawyers come in all stripes, and they twist the truth every which way but up."

"Not in my case."

I stopped in my tracks. "The house slid down the hill."

He got in my face. "Because my subcontractor cut corners when he drilled into the hill to install the support beams for the house. Instead of going twenty feet down, he only went ten. He also used cheap cement to anchor them. It was full of sand and practically melted in that monsoon we had. He made a killing off not just me, but a bunch of other contractors and then skipped to Rio. I proved it, and it's a matter of public record."

I gaped. Then I scoffed. "If that's the case, then why does your name still reek of old fish in the Seattle business community?"

He ground his teeth. I saw his cheek muscles flex.

"I'm the one who uncovered the subcontractor's rip-off." His voice came out as tight as those muscles. "I pulled the plug on a scam that took in some of the area's major players. They hate to look gullible, so they resent me for naming them as fellow dupes. That kind of thing puts a damper on referrals."

He could be telling the truth. Then again, this could be the smoke screen he and his lawyer had cooked up. "I reserve the right to doubt you, if you don't mind."

"That's what the masses in Seattle decided to do."

I'd hit the nail on the head. He felt he'd been treated unfairly because of what someone else had done. Hmm . . . sounded familiar. I could wind up paying for someone else's crime if things didn't go my way.

"You have a valid point." I resumed my walk toward my car. "But you still haven't said what you were doing at Marge's house."

He gave me a sideways look. "You still see it as Marge's house?"

"Of course it's Marge's house. Whose would it be? Steve can't even pay taxes on the place with his teacher's salary."

"Has it occurred to you that, as Marge's heir, the house will be yours as soon as it clears probate?" Green eyes raked me. "Either you're really, really good, or you're innocent."

My ears buzzed. I felt dizzy. I swayed, then fought to regain control. I couldn't let him see how he'd affected me. "That house hasn't crossed my mind, not for one single moment. So that makes me really good at what?"

"At deflecting suspicion."

"So we're back to your stupid accusation. Maybe it's obsession. I told you once, and I'll tell you again: I didn't kill Marge."

I didn't know whether his eyes were icy or fiery green, but I did know they gave me the willies.

He finally said, "You could be telling the truth, but as I said, you could also be a very, very good actress."

"Okay. This chat's over."

I ran to my Honda and started it up.

To my right, Dutch got into a dented blue pickup. Then he just sat, his green eyes boring holes in me. To get away from that stare, I pulled out of my parking spot and into traffic.

He followed.

I hurried home. The *eau de* ripe refuse was getting to me. The thought of a long, sudsy shower exerted a powerful pull. But no matter how fast I drove or how many off-the-wall turns I took, Dutch stuck to my rear bumper like lint to cheap upholstery.

When I pulled into the driveway, he did the same. His truck blocked the sidewalk. Now I was mad.

I marched up to the crummy truck. "What do you think you're doing, you lunatic? It's against the law to park your tank in the path of pedestrians. Get it out of here."

He stepped down from the cab.

I slammed my fists on my hips, and my backpack purse banged my right knee. "Okay. So why don't you tell me what you *really* want?"

"I want you to confess so the cops can lock you up and I can get on with my life."

I refused to dignify that with an answer. I headed for the porch.

"You know," he said, "it'd go easier on you if you did confess. I'm sure you could plea-bargain your way out of the death penalty—maybe they'd go for life without parole."

I didn't pause. But at that point, my lousy luck took another turn downward. A familiar gray streak flew at me and latched on to the hem of my trash-slimed pants. Bali H'ai had an unrivaled reputation for dumpster diving. I guess I smelled enough like a dumpster for her to ignore the small differences between a huge metal receptacle and me.

"Bella!" I hollered. She lived across the street and one house over from the manse. At this time of day, she liked to have a cup of tea in her too-busy living room, and since her windows were wide open, I was pretty sure she could hear me. "Come get your demented cat before I call animal control."

No matter which way I turned my ankle, the miserable feline hung on for dear life. I was careful not to hurt her, but I also had to look out for my own tender skin.

I remembered Dutch. "Don't just stand there—do something!"

Only then did I hear his laugh. Ducky. Just peachy dandy. Every woman should aspire to make a suspicious madman's day more fun.

"What do you want me to do?" he asked between barks of mirth.

"You can quit yucking and take this creature off me."

He laughed some more. "Hey, I told you I have a healthy sense of self-preservation. I'm not messing with that cat. It seems to have found its bliss."

"Oh dear," Bella cried from across the street. "Bali H'ai, you naughty girl. How'd you get out?"

She couldn't be serious. "Bella. Your windows are wide open, and half of them don't have screens. What do think a cat's going to do? Just sit there and swish her tail?"

Bella trotted over. "That's just what she does."

Bali H'ai wrestled my pant leg. The mega rats at Marge's wouldn't have stood a chance with her. "No way. She goes AWOL all the time. How many times have the neighbors complained about their overturned trash?"

"That isn't my baby." Bella squatted by my embattled foot. "She's too delicate for such behavior—" She wrinkled her pink nose. "Haley!"

Yeah, yeah. And Bali H'ai is sensitive. "You were saying? Your cat made a beeline for me the minute she got a whiff of this. And I'm pretty disgusting right about now."

Dutch howled.

I glared. "Come on, guys. Have mercy. Not only am I swathed in slop, but I also stink and am sticky, and this cat's ripping my pants."

Bella backed away, her hand over her nose. "I can't stand the smell. What have you been up to?"

Dutch smirked. "She went snoo—"

"I had an accident!" It was rude to interrupt, but Bella didn't need more ideas. "I . . . um . . . tripped over some trash. Now please take the cat so I can clean up. Please."

Something in my tone must have penetrated Dutch's mirth, because he bent and took hold of Bali H'ai's middle.

"Haley?" Dad called from the front porch. "Are you okay?"

Then everything went to the dogs—literally. Midas ran out and spotted Bali H'ai. He barked for the sheer joy of finding a cat on his front lawn. In his opinion, as we'd learned in the past, that made the cat fair game.

He barreled toward Bali H'ai. The builder got in his way. Dutch fell.

Bali H'ai yowled, puffed up like a soft porcupine, and shot away in a blur of gray.

I made for the porch. "Come on, Midas."

Unfortunately, Midas was out for fresh cat. He took off after Bella's monster, his leash trailing in his wake.

Bali H'ai crossed the street.

Midas followed.

A car turned the corner.

"No!" I screamed, frozen by panic.

As fast as Bali H'ai had fled, Dutch ran after my dog and planted his big sneakered foot on the leather leash. Midas jerked to a stop inches from the fender.

Suddenly silence.

No more cat yowls.

No more barks.

No more squealing tires.

"You seem to have a knack for strange incidents, Ms. Farrell."

I hadn't noticed Detective Tsu's arrival, but I couldn't miss her now. She stood a mere ten feet away.

I sighed. "And you're here to make this one even more so, right?"

"That depends on your answer to my question."

"Hmm . . . was I clairvoyant or what?"

Her perfectly curved eyebrow rose. "About . . . ?"

"I predicted you'd have more questions for me, didn't I?"

"It's my job, and I'm good at it."

I dropped my backpack purse, crossed my arms, and came near. I chuckled when she tried not to grimace. My horrific stench struck again. Maybe it would shorten the inquisition. "Ask away."

"Here?" She looked from Dad to Dutch, who held Midas's leash and with his free hand scratched a doggy ear, and then to Bella.

I shrugged. "I told you I'm innocent. I have nothing to hide."

The detective unzipped her fancy handbag and pulled out her notebook and silver pen. "Where would Marge Norwalk's Rolodex be?"

Marge's business relied on the industrial-sized address thingy. "Last I saw it, it sat on her desk at the warehouse. Is it missing?"

"My question makes that quite clear."

"Well, I don't know where else it could be."

"Did you take it?"

"Why would I?"

"Because you might want to cull potential clients."

"I wouldn't need to take the thing. Marge had begun to refer me."

Detective Tsu tapped the notebook with her pen. "Any idea who else might have an interest in those addresses?"

"Not really, but I suppose a rival auctioneer might want to lure her regulars."

"That's always possible."

"I assume you think it has something to do with the murder."

"The timing's certainly interesting."

"Are you sure it disappeared after Marge died?"

"According to Mr. Krieger, it was there the day of the sale. Two days later when he went to contact absentee bidders, it was gone."

Ozzie. Again. I took a step closer. "Has it occurred to you, while you try to pin a murder on me I didn't commit, that Ozzie could be the killer?"

The detective drew in a sharp breath and wrinkled her nose.

She said, "I'm not trying to pin anything on you, and I'm a thorough investigator. I follow every lead. Unfortunately, the evidence leads back to you."

"Then get busy and find new leads. You're wrong about me."

"I'll do what I have to do. When I'm done, I'll have the killer."

"Again," I insisted, "you should look at people who might have wanted Marge dead. Like her husband and Ozzie Krieger." And Noreen, but I wasn't ready to tell Ms. Tsu that just yet.

"We've checked on them, and I can assure you, we were thorough. We now need the Rolodex. If you should remember seeing it elsewhere . . ." Her eyes did that laser thing of hers. I didn't squirm.

She went on. "If you remember anything, don't hesitate to call."

Who would? "If I find anything that'll prove you wrong, believe me, I won't wait to tell you who, what, when, where, why, and how."

Like the last time, her laughter surprised me. "I'll just bet you won't, Ms. Farrell. Have a good afternoon." She followed her words with a look that swept me head to toe. "You might want to do something about the salad. It makes a fashion statement, but it's not you."

Against my better judgment, I laughed. "You know? Maybe Tyler was right. You might not be so bad after all."

The detective smiled. She stowed her notebook and pen in her bag, then paused to rub Midas behind his right ear. The turncoat dropped and rolled onto his back. She knelt at his side, tickled his belly, and chuckled when his rear left leg waved rhythmically.

"I should get a new dog," she said when she stood. "Please let me know if you hear of pups from his stock. He's a great guy."

I watched her drive away, not sure what to make of the enigmatic detective. Was she investigating as thoroughly as she said? Or was she doing the rush-to-judgment thing the media said happened so much?

I didn't have long to ponder the question. Dutch held out Midas's leash. "He is a great dog. Even though his owner leaves something to be desired in the law-abiding department."

"Hey! I'm innocent until proven guilty, and I won't be—proven guilty, that is—because I didn't kill Marge."

"The lead detective seems pretty suspicious."

What was it with these people and their knifelike stares? I turned away. "How do I know you're not accusing me because, for some pea-brained reason, you decided to kill Marge?"

"Give me a break. I didn't even know the woman. Besides, I need that money-pit house to sell—to Noreen, in particular. Now I'm stuck waiting until the cops let the sale go ahead. I'm the last guy who'd want to kill the auctioneer."

Dad had obviously had enough. "I normally espouse hospitality, but I have to ask you to leave. You have no idea how absurd your accusation is. My daughter loved Marge like a mother, and she would never have harmed her. Now, Haley needs a bath—"

"She does," Dutch said. "And I'll leave, but I have a stake in this investigation. I'm not about to let anyone ruin my chance to get back on my feet. Not your daughter nor anyone else."

"I heard your first threat," I muttered on my way to the porch. "You didn't scare me then, and you don't scare me now. I have nothing to worry about."

Sure, I didn't. I wouldn't be the first innocent to wind up in jail. But I wasn't going to give an inch. Not to him.

I'd talk to Steve tomorrow, Noreen or no Noreen.

I arrived at the ritzy Carleton-Higgins Academy at 11:50. Summer school ran only in the morning, as I'd learned when I'd phoned the school's office under false pretenses earlier that morning. Sort of. I did want to deliver something, a bunch of questions to a guy who now made my stomach turn.

Steve had been cheating on Marge, and with Noreen, no less. The entire sexual scenario made me sick, and I knew it'd be hard to face the man who'd treated my mentor so shabbily.

What about Noreen? Was she involved with Dutch too? How could I work for her now that I knew what she'd been up to behind Marge's back? What she—the other woman—might have done to Steve's wife.

But I couldn't think about that yet. I had to focus. I had to find out if Steve had really been out of town the day Marge died. I had to find out how badly Steve had wanted Noreen . . . enough to kill?

When kids spilled out the sleek glass doors of the expensive school building, I stepped out of my car and stood in the shade of a tall tree. I wasn't known for my patience, but this mattered. It mattered a lot, so I made myself wait until the suave blond that Marge had married two years ago, to all her friends' shock, came out.

"Steve!"

He turned. "Haley. I'm surprised to see you. Did you need me?"

I saw him differently now. Yes, he was GQ handsome, but almost too much so. He styled his hair to perfection—a strike against him in the eyes of someone with imperfect hair. I shoved a wild bunch behind my ear.

Something about the expensive summer-weight wool pants and the silk shirt also bothered me. I'd never caught on to his extravagance before.

I shifted my weight. "I've some questions for you."

His expression changed. "I don't have to answer."

"You might want to answer mine before they become the police's."

"What? You're playing cops and robbers now?"

"I'm trying to save my skin. The lead detective has me in her crosshairs, and I don't particularly want to go to jail."

"If you did the crime, you'll just have to do the time . . . or something like that."

"Give me a break, Steve. You know I had nothing to do with Marge's death." *Okay. Courage, please.* With the help of some of Tyler's techniques, I focused. "The philandering husband might have a good reason to knock off his wife."

He hadn't expected that. With a look over his left shoulder, he took a step back. "I didn't kill Marge."

"I didn't either, so knock off the stupid blame game. Did Marge, *your wife*, crimp your style with Noreen? Was she in the way?"

"That's stupid, and I don't have to answer."

"You might want the practice. I'm sure the cops'll ask some of the same things." I took a deep breath. "Did you want Noreen more than Marge?"

"Look, I married Marge. That should count for something."

"Ah . . . counting does come in handy when money's involved, doesn't it? So you decided you wanted Noreen but didn't want to give up Marge's money to marry her."

Steve laughed. "I don't want to marry Noreen. I'm not that crazy. Pity the man who ties himself up to that shark."

He got sleazier by the minute. "Then where were you the day of the auction?"

"At a conference in Detroit. A teacher's conference."

"Can you prove it?"

He smirked. "I have an airline ticket, hotel receipt, and registration materials—"

"Woo-hoo!" a rusty-haired kid called from behind Steve's right. "Mr. Norwalk's got another harem babe. Kissy, kissy, kissy!"

A sneer did nothing for Steve's looks. "Robert, that's awfully rude. This is a friend of my late wife. Please apologize."

"Why? Class's out, and she's just one more of your women."

Robert looked to be about fourteen and a rotten deal. But what he said caught my attention. "Is Mr. Norwalk a favorite with the ladies, then?"

"No joke." He ticked off fingers—and ticked off his teacher too. "There's Miss Collins from the English department, and Sienna's mom—she's divorced now—plus, he married the older one." He shot Steve a malevolent leer. "There's the one with the blue eyes, the Jag, and the killer bod, and now you. That's five I know of. Betcha he's got more."

I watched Steve. "Interesting . . ."

He practically spewed steam. "Nonsense. Robert just flunked his geometry test." He turned to the teen. "This won't change your grade. It'd be better if you applied your mind to your homework and studied for the next test. Don't waste time on tall tales."

Robert shrugged. "I know what I see."

"And what would that be?" asked a gentleman in a gray suit.

Robert gulped. "Mr. Hobart . . . I didn't see you there. I . . . ah . . ."

"Go on, Robert. I'd like to hear what you have to say."

The venom in Steve's gaze made me gasp. Who was Mr. Hobart?

"Well, sir," Robert said, "it's just that every time I turn around, Mr. Norwalk's got another of his women hanging around. He's a big-time player, ya know?"

I winced. My opinion of Steve had taken a dive when I'd seen him with Noreen the previous afternoon, but this was embarrassing. Sympathy rose in me—just a little. He was reaping what he'd sown.

"I . . . see . . ." Mr. Hobart turned to me. "Let me introduce myself. I'm Edward Hobart, headmaster here at the Carleton-Higgins Academy. And unfortunately for you, I know who you are, Ms. Farrell. Your picture's been in the paper a time or two these last few days."

I grimaced. "Notoriety's a bear."

"I would imagine." He turned to Robert. "You'd better hurry. Your sister's waiting, and I know she starts work at one."

Robert took off, a gangly mess of arms, legs, and floppy red hair. Before I could think of a thing to say, Mr. Hobart went on.

"I'm going to have to say good-bye, Ms. Farrell. I need to see Mr. Norwalk in my office."

That fast, I took over Robert's place as the target at which my mentor's widower shot visual darts of hate.

8

Did I affect people or what?

After that splendid encounter with Steve, I went home and, since I needed income, pulled out the photos of the Stokers' living and dining rooms. I took the pictures and my rulers, colored pencils, paint-chip fan, and box of sample fabrics to the kitchen, where I spread everything out on the table.

With a cup of Starbucks in one hand and a Milky Way bar in the other, I plopped on a chair and stared at the stuff of my brand-new career. I should have been excited about my first professional project, but instead, Marge's death consumed my thoughts and emotions.

I munched a mouthful of candy and tried to envision Gussie's rooms emptied of their current furnishings. I failed.

Had Steve killed Marge? If so, had he done it alone, or had he enlisted Noreen?

After what I saw yesterday, anything was possible.

Yesterday . . . what a day.

I'd avoided philosophical waxing for years, but yesterday taught me a couple of unexpected lessons.

When I propped my chin on my hand, the empty candy wrapper dropped to the floor. Midas's indelicate slurps followed. I bent, snatched the messy paper away, balled it, and tossed it into the garbage.

I now had a new understanding of trash. Before yesterday I wouldn't have thought I'd find rich people's garbage overrun by rats. But I had, and I'd figured out something else. No matter how much money a person has in the bank, most also have stuff in their lives they don't want disturbed, personal repulsive rodents in their trash sheds.

I figured Steve's women were among his. Not that the women themselves were rats necessarily, just his adulterous ways. I wondered what else might lurk in his back shed.

The second thing I learned is that information comes in odd packages. A mouthy fourteen-year-old isn't your typical informant, but I learned more about Steve from Robert than during years of acquaintance and from his late wife.

What I still didn't know was if he'd killed Marge.

I suspected him now more than I had before I knew of his affair with Noreen. I'd thought Noreen was romantically tied to Dutch. Yesterday's discovery made me more uneasy than ever.

Did Noreen have something to gain by killing Marge? Beyond getting Steve all to herself, that is. And how did Dutch figure into all this? Was Noreen in love with him? Did she really care for Steve instead? Or—yuck—was she playing with both men?

In spite of my disgust, I had to look into these sticky matters. Did I ever wish I didn't have to. But if I wanted to avoid jail, I needed my questions answered.

And what was Ozzie's part in this puzzle?

I would've been better off if I'd studied criminology instead of interior design.

When the phone rang, I didn't know whether to gripe at the interruption or to cheer. Noreen was on the other end.

"I'd like to meet with you and Dutch now that you've both had a chance to see the Gerrity mansion," she said.

Mention of the house brought back the memory of Marge's body, its life spent, my friend gone. I still didn't know if I could work with Noreen after all that had happened, but the least I could do was go. Oh, and get a handle on my emotions too.

"When would you like to do that?" I asked.

"As soon as possible. Are you busy tomorrow morning . . . say around nine thirty?"

Aside from the Stoker project, I had nothing else on my plate, and Noreen knew it. "I'm available."

"Then how about if we meet here at my condo. Do you need directions?"

I knew the ultraluxurious development. But as we made small talk, an idea occurred to me. "Would you mind if I came a few minutes early? I have a color-chip fan, and I doubt Dutch is interested in color schemes."

That wasn't a flat-out lie. I do have the fan, and I was pretty sure Dutch didn't want to see it, but I had no intention of simply bringing out the color chips when I met with Noreen. I also had questions for her.

"That'd be great!"

Noreen really wanted that place. Would she have killed Marge, and in the process put the brakes on her purchase? I hoped to find out. Soon.

"Then how about if I get there about fifteen or twenty minutes earlier? Maybe more like nine-ish?"

"Oh, I can't wait!" Noreen sounded like a teen headed for a heartthrob's concert instead of a thirtysomething widow. "What do you like? Coffee? Tea? Bagels or croissants? I'll make sure to have something fun to eat while we choose colors. That'll be fun."

I gulped. She made it sound as if we'd be doing some kind of morning pajama party. I only wanted to delve into her secrets . . . her trash shed, so to speak. "I'm a Starbucks fan, but it's not necessary, and bagels are great."

"They'll be ready at nine. Thanks so much, Haley. I just know the house is going to be wonderful."

She hung up, and I held the receiver a couple of minutes longer. What had Dutch said the morning of the auction? Hadn't he warned Noreen against counting unhatched chickens? Maybe she was innocent. I didn't think a killer would expect cops to let the sale go through any time soon.

I returned the phone to its cradle, and it dawned on me that I'd really scored. I'd have Noreen to my nosy self for at least a half hour before Dutch arrived.

"Cha-ching!" I pumped my fist in victory. "Bingo!"

I did a little victory dance back to my chair. Midas opened one eye, clearly bewildered by my sudden activity. "Hey, you know? I might be on to something here. I coulda been great, I coulda been a champion . . . a contender . . . something like that!"

Midas yawned.

Yeah, I can be goofy, but I haven't been for a long time. Still, I couldn't let that take over my thoughts. I'd stuck my foot in Noreen's door, and I was going to celebrate.

Tomorrow might turn into another fiasco along the lines of yesterday, but I was taking my fun while I could.

"Goal!" I crowed. Hey, if soccer players on Spanish-language TV channels could go bonkers when they scored, so could I. I'd never understood the fuss when the ball did what it was supposed to do. Now I had a new appreciation for success.

I just hoped it carried me through to the killer's conviction.

When I stepped into Noreen's condo, I knew I was in over my head. I'd studied all kinds of decorating styles and knew how much furnishings cost, but this place went beyond intimidating. From the high-gloss black marble floor, to the white silk fabric on the walls, to the avant-garde gray stone sculpture on the custom steel credenza in the entry, to the low white leather couch that lined two walls—made to order, of course—the place reeked of jet-set budget.

I come from the steal-of-a-deal end of the spectrum.

What do I know about this kind of taste? After all, I'm the one who named my business Decorating $ense. It doesn't make sense to me to go into hock just to get a home to look nice.

Noreen doesn't share my philosophy.

"Make yourself comfortable," she trilled on her way to the kitchen. "I'll be right back with our goodies."

Comfortable? Here?

Hah!

I tucked my backpack under the endless glass coffee table and unzipped my portfolio. I had to at least make it look as though I'd really come to discuss colors and whatnot. I spread out my fabric swatches, and thank goodness I had some nice dupioni and raw silks, some knobby linens, and spectacular cashmere wool in the mix. I could imagine the look Noreen would have given me if I'd pulled out my favorite muslins, chambrays, simple chenilles, or—yikes!—cotton in prints or even ticking stripes.

At least I don't do fake, man-made, pseudofabric stuff.

"Here you go," my maybe client said. "Help yourself."

She set the silver tray on the glass surface, and trust me, there was plenty of room in spite of my mess. I noticed the quality cut-crystal goblets of orange juice—fresh squeezed, since bits of plump pulp floated on top.

Not only did she offer bagels and the usual cream cheese, but on a paper-thin platinum and white porcelain plate sat glorious slices of smoked salmon. An antique jelly jar, cut crystal to match the goblets, held jewel-toned preserves, and the handle of what looked like a honey stirrer poked out of a superb silver pot.

My gaping jaw nearly clipped the glass table.

"You didn't have to go to so much trouble," I said. "This is wonderful though."

"It was nothing. My housekeeper loves good food, so she had a ball putting it together." She sipped orange juice, then pointed at the fabrics with the goblet. "These look nice. Where would you use them?"

I gulped down my bite of salmon-draped bagel. "I didn't have a particular place in mind. I brought them to see what you like."

With a tiny silver fork, Noreen picked up a translucent orange curl of fish. She rolled it up, popped it into her mouth, and chewed, an appreciative smile on her face. "Naomi outdid herself with this salmon."

I couldn't talk with a full mouth, so I nodded.

Noreen continued. "Anyway. I like all kinds of things, but I insist on feel-good fabrics and upholstery. I want only the best against my skin. I can't stand those trendy burlaps and scratchy stuff. Give me a slinky silk any day."

I knew where to take this chat next. "What about colors?"

She wrinkled her nose. "I'm just so done with all this white stuff on black stuff, you know?"

I nodded again.

"I want to surround myself with sultry, rich jewel tones. I think they make a woman look younger, sexier."

My eyes nearly bugged out. She'd been having an affair with a married man, now formerly married, and maybe with a handsome bad-boy builder too, and she thought she needed colors on her walls to make her more appealing?

I was so out of my league.

"Why don't you show me what colors you like?"

Noreen flipped through the color chips. She tipped her head one way then the next, intent, focused, sipping juice every so often. This seemed as good a time as any to launch my attack.

"Did Marge know about you and Steve?"

The goblet fell. Chips of glass flew into the cream cheese. Juice splashed on the white leather. Noreen's eyes blazed cobalt fire.

"What do you mean?"

I laughed. I was nervous, and her outraged look hit me funny. "Don't take me for a fool. Did Marge know you were having an affair with her husband?"

The color on Noreen's cheeks matched the preserves, which I still hadn't tried and, even though they looked good, probably never would now.

"I want you to decorate my new home, not stick your nose in my private life."

"I'm not sticking my nose in your private life. I'm asking a question about something that could affect my future. I'm sure you know the police think I killed Marge."

"Do you think I killed Marge? For Steve?" Her smile wasn't nice.

"I just asked a question. Did Marge know you were having an affair with her husband?"

Her glare intensified.

The doorbell rang.

That would be the other man in Noreen's life. I didn't know how involved she was with Dutch.

"I'll be right back," Noreen said between clenched teeth. It didn't sound polite or like a promise. It struck me as a threat.

At this rate, I'd be dismembered before I found out who'd killed my friend.

"You're here already?" Dutch asked a minute later.

What could I say? I went with the obvious. "Evidently."

"I hope you haven't come up with structural changes for the place. You'll have to wait until I check out the whole building before you consider anything like that."

"I brought paint chips and fabrics to see what Noreen likes—"

"She came to ask nosy questions," our would-be employer said. "I hope you're not loaded for bear too."

Dutch gave me a dark look. "I came to talk about the Gerrity mansion. What's your deal?"

"Can't help it if I want to stay out of jail."

He groaned. "What'd you do now?"

"I need to know how Noreen felt about sharing Steve with Marge."

Dutch's green eyes opened wider. "Are you crazy?"

"I'm as sane as the next guy." My perch on the white leather sofa left me at a distinct disadvantage, so I stood. "You'd both want to know if you were in my shoes."

Noreen sneered. "I'd never get into a mess like yours."

"And I'd never corner someone I thought might be a killer on my own," Dutch added. "You'd be surprised how short your life can get if you ask the wrong person the wrong question at the wrong time."

Noreen turned her anger on him. "I'm not a killer, and I resent what you just said. I sat next to you the whole sale. When would I have had the chance to kill Marge Norwalk? Even if I'd wanted to, which I didn't. Divorce is less messy."

Dutch jabbed a long finger my way. "I didn't say you did. She's the one acting like Nancy Drew."

When her glare bounced back at me, I dropped into Noreen's bad graces again. Not that I'd ever left. "Are you so desperate that you'll accuse anyone you think of?" she said. "If that's the case, then you probably did kill Marge."

"Give me a break! Would I care about the redesign of the Gerrity if I'd killed Marge? If I had, I'd be pretty happy to keep the place shut down for good. Besides, asking tough questions isn't the best way to land a job. If I'd wanted money or whatever, I wouldn't need to work for you anymore now, would I?"

Ooh . . . that didn't come out right.

Dutch groaned again. "Okay. This meeting's over." He took my elbow and dragged me toward the door. "We'll get together another time, Noreen. Sometime after Haley takes her meds."

"Hey! I only take vitamins." I pulled out of his clutches. "And I haven't asked all my questions yet."

"Oh, yes you have." He came up and wrapped his arm around my waist. "At least for today."

I darted to the side. "Noreen hasn't answered. I wonder why. What's she hiding?"

When Noreen gasped, I went in for the kill. "Did Marge catch you and Steve . . . umm . . . together?"

"No!" Noreen cried. "Are you happy now?"

Dutch clapped his big hands on my shoulders and pushed me to the door. "Now you have your answer. Let's get out of here before she calls security."

I yanked away. "Don't manhandle me!"

"Don't mess up my life any more than you already have."

"I haven't."

"You have."

Noreen darted between us. She opened the door. "Good-bye!"

We walked out. On the slate step outside, I turned. "I have another question—"

She slammed the door.

"How rude." I headed for the car but came to a screeching halt partway there. "I left my stuff. She can't keep my bag and my samples. I need them for work."

Dutch rolled his eyes. "I'll get them. I don't think she wants to see you again any time soon."

Whether I liked it or not, I had to agree. I'd bungled that. And unless he managed to sweet-talk Noreen into forking over my things, I'd be in a heap of trouble. To begin with, my driver's license was in my bag. Oh, and the Honda keys too.

I stood in the driveway and looked at my little car and then at the European models in driveways up and down the street. I'd learned another lesson, one that didn't surprise me.

Wealth did nothing for me; it didn't impress or daunt me.

So much for the momentary intimidation I'd felt when I'd walked into Noreen's place.

But this wasn't the time to ruminate on my condition. Dutch came out, my backpack purse over one vast shoulder, my portfolio clutched to his chest. A scrap of fuchsia silk clung to the hint of stubble already visible on his shaven chin.

The absurdity of the moment didn't escape my notice. I laughed.

He frowned. "What's wrong with you?"

"Nothing," I said between chuckles. "Everything . . . *you*!"

"Oh, that's clear."

He had no clue how funny he looked, and I figured I'd be better off if it stayed that way. "Here. I'll take my things and head on home."

"Chalk this one up as another failure, will ya?"

"Oh, I don't know. There's something to be said for starting your day off with a laugh."

He gave me a grimace on steroids. "I didn't hear that," he muttered. "I didn't hear a thing."

"Good-bye, Dutch." I threw my stuff in the backseat of my car and slid behind the wheel. "Look at the bright side."

His green eyes opened wider. "There's a bright side?"

"Sure."

"And that would be . . . ?"

"Noreen didn't fire us."

He groaned. "Yet."

I gave him a valiant chuckle and drove away. He was right. Noreen hadn't fired us yet. But she could at any minute.

And she probably would by the time I got home. I didn't want to see the answering machine in the kitchen. The flashing red light, which usually drew me like a moth, would stop me dead in my tracks.

I might just have dealt my career a deathblow before it had a chance to live. And I might just have given the killer a heads-up.

That criminology course looked better by the minute, if for no other reason than to learn how to stay a step ahead of the creep who'd already killed once.

Hours of recrimination later, I gave Gussie a golden retriever look. It got me nowhere. "Why can't you?"

"Because I showed you how to lead a meeting the last time."

"But this isn't a real meeting—it's not Saturday morning."

"The missionary society scheduled this presentation two months ago, and as the new president, you need to introduce our guest. Go ahead. Get the ball rolling."

"The only thing that's going to roll is my stupid head." I took my place behind the podium. This was almost worse than the morning's escapade had been. Or maybe it was my just deserts.

With another mock glare at Gussie, who only chuckled, I picked up the gavel and gave it a whack. The room fell silent. Good grief! Who'd have thought I'd have that kind of power?

"Ah . . . hi."

I winced at my stellar eloquence. I tried again. "Hi, ladies. Um . . . Gussie tells me Mr. Bowersox is here to tell us about raising money by selling telephone calling cards."

The gray gent—he was as gray as a human could be: gray hair, gray eyes, gray suit, even gray skin—nodded glumly.

Swell. He even had a gray disposition.

I blundered forward. "Since I can't figure out how anyone could make money selling phone cards, I guess it's best if Mr. Graysocks . . . er . . . Bowersox comes and tells us."

Silence.

Shocked women.

A snigger in the back of the crowd.

Finally, Gussie shook her head and began to clap.

The speaker came and, thankfully, took my place behind the podium. I fled faster than Bali H'ai ever had. For the next hour and a half, I took refuge behind the mammoth silk weeping fig in a corner of the church's community room and ignored the occasional stare sent my way.

Something had to give. At the rate I was going, I'd be either bashed in the head by Marge's killer, banned from my father's church, or both before the end of the week.

Applying a hot-glue gun to shut my mouth seemed like a good idea.

Eventually, the dull monologue came to an end. I returned
to the podium, told everyone where the refreshments were
(as if they, longtime members of the church, didn't know
where they'd left the cookies, fruit breads, and punch) and
said good night to one and all.

Gussie blocked my escape. "You can't leave yet. The president leaves last."

Was this day ever going to end? I wondered if I could talk
Tyler into opening the *dojo* for me. There was something about
a good punching bag . . .

But escape didn't come easy. Oh, no. Not for me.

Bella marched up. "I've a bone to pick with you, chickie. You
said you'd let me help when you went sleuthing, and you've been
up to some pretty cool stuff. But you didn't tell me a thing!"

Who'd told her about my calamities?

"I haven't done anything that would interest you, Bella."

"You wanna make a bet?" She crossed her pudgy arms
over her cotton-candy-pink top. "Lorrianne Dumont saw you
skulking in Marge's trash yesterday. She says you had some
major hunk with you. Is that the hottie who squished my poor
Bali H'ai? I wouldn't share him either, but you promised I
could help you snoop."

"I've never skulked." I felt safe with that. I'd made enough
noise to wake up rocks in Outer Slobovia.

Bella's blue eyes narrowed to slits. "You sure stunk of
trash."

"I told you I'd tripped over some stinky stuff."

"In Marge's trash."

"It wasn't Marge's." Marge had been dead for a few days.
It was probably Steve's.

"I'd have done better'n you did if you'd taken me along to snoop around."

She probably would have. I doubt anyone could do worse. "I . . . ah . . . snooping's not part of my business."

True again.

"Now, Bella," Gussie said. "Let the poor girl go. She's had some rough days, and she doesn't need this. I'm sure she'll include you at the right time."

Bella's eyes filled with tears. "Oh, honey. Just listen to me. You lost your friend, and all I can do is carp like a vulture about snooping and clues. Here, let me give you a hug."

I nearly broke down and cried. In spite of her nuttiness, Bella was as good as the proverbial gold. "I promise," I whispered into her pink mane. "I promise I'll bring you with me when I can use your help."

That seemed to satisfy her, since she went home a short while later. I sat on the nearest chair and refused to let a single thought take root.

Finally, the last three ladies left. It was just Gussie and me and the chairs in the room.

"Are you going to be okay?" she asked.

"Someday." The quiver in my voice bothered me.

"You know you can count on me, don't you?"

"Always, Gussie."

"Good." She rolled up and placed a hand on my arm. "I know it's hard to lose someone, and you've had two hard blows. Please call if you need anything. We can talk. I can make a pot of Starbucks. I can give you a hug. I love you, Haley."

"I love you too, Gussie. And thanks. Thanks for being you."

Feeling less alone, I locked up the church's auxiliary building and then watched Tom Stoker gently ease his disabled wife into the passenger seat of their van.

I was fortunate to have had Marge when my life imploded on me—twice, no less. And now it seemed that another wonderful woman wanted to help me through this latest rough patch. I'd be a real basket case if I had to go it alone. What would life be like without people like Dad and Marge and Gussie?

I walked home, more determined than ever to do my best in her home. She deserved no less from me.

I'd just have to be more discreet in my investigation. Even though it might be smarter to quit my efforts, I wasn't sure I was ready to trust the cops.

I didn't want to go to jail. Not when I had jobs the Stokers and maybe even Noreen were willing to pay me to do.

Marge's killer wouldn't get away with murder.

I had too much to lose.

9

Satisfied with my initial drawings for the Stokers, I packed my portfolio and headed to Magnus Mills by ten the next morning. I wasn't going to think about Marge's murder until I had a finished design board for the Stokers.

I learned to love the design-board concept at school. I get a kick out of seeing my suggestions spread out on a large piece of foam core. I attach fabric samples and paint chips around the floor plan I set in the center, and in the corners of the board I include photos of furniture pieces that might work in the room. This is the fun part, the idea and its development. Purchasing and installation are pure hard work and fraught with monumental roadblocks and headaches.

Today I was off to one of my favorite places. Adrienne Magnus Soames, great-granddaughter of Orville Magnus, founder of the mill, is a fabric genius. Orville had established a weaving facility. On Adrienne's persistent advice, his grandson Craig, her father, began to import some unique fabrics. Now semiretired, Craig gave his business- and art-savvy daughter the reins to the business. She gave the company wings. Thanks to Adrienne's army of buyers, Magnus Mills has taken its place as a powerhouse in the fabric world. They now offer woven material from every corner of the world at bargain prices. Adrienne pays producers a fair price, then resells based on what she paid, not on an inflated snob scale designed to stroke the ego of pretentious designers du jour.

I love Adrienne and her wares.

"Haley!" Adrienne said when I walked into her kaleidoscopic warehouse. "How're you doing?"

She had to stoop to hug me. Despite her six-foot height, she had yet to give up the four-inch heels she fell for during her time on the silver screen. I would have fallen too. On my face.

I mumbled into her collarbone, "I'm okay, as okay as possible."

Adrienne held me away, scoured me head to toe, then shook her glossy, prematurely pewter-grayed head. "You look wonderful, considering."

"You mean I don't look like something the cat dragged in?"

"Of course not."

"I should, considering."

Adrienne crossed her arms and gave me a disgusted look.

"Hey," I said, "I was attacked by a demented cat. She did everything in her power to drag me to her owner as the trophy of the year. See, I'd been hanging with rats—you know, the gross kind with long, hairless tails."

Even when she wrinkles her perfect, elegant nose, Adrienne looks spectacular. "I'm sure I don't want to know more." She shuddered. "Rats, Haley? Please."

"Tell you what. You show me your most fabulous loot, and I won't mention rodents again."

The ridiculously elongated and outrageously pointed toe of one of her glamour-girl shoes tapped a time or two. "On its face, your offer seems too good to pass up, but you did a job on my curiosity. I've an even better offer for you, and I don't think you can pass it up. Tell me about the cat and the rats, and I'll up your discount."

"You know me, Adrienne. I don't like to dump on anyone."

"Oh, honey, you know you can talk to me. Your mom, Marge, and I go back a long, long time. You even used to call me Auntie Adie when you were little."

"You weren't that big then either. You and Marge are at least eight years younger than Mom, and she had me when she was only twenty-two."

Adrienne looked down her nose. Nobody does it better than she, a good reason why she'd made such a splash in Hollywood. "It's never a calendar thing, Haley. Maturity is a state of mind."

"Sure. We live in Washington. Talk about a state of mind."

We laughed on our way to the stacks. I recounted—with some wise edits—my exploits of the past two days. Marge's death had devastated Adrienne too. They'd been friends nearly forever. She'd called me on my cell phone while I sat in gridlocked traffic on the way back from my meeting with my favorite shyster, Mr. Harris, the day after Marge's murder. We'd cried, comforted each other, and failed to make sense of the senseless crime.

"Now that you gave me a stitch in the side," the material

maven said at the end of my tale of indignity, "why don't you tell me what you're looking for."

I showed her my floor plan and the case goods I hoped Gussie would approve. "I'd like to contrast the warm walnut tone of these wood tables, new entertainment center, and shelving units with something in an equally warm but more neutral palette."

Adrienne shot me a look of horror. "You're doing beige?"

I laughed. "No way! I was thinking along the lines of rich caramel, mellow gold, some buttercream, and maybe a hit or two of persimmon to keep things from looking too tame."

"Phew!" Adrienne was not a neutral sort. "Let's go for the gold on the sofa with this supersoft chenille, and for the draperies, I have the most delicious caramel-sundae dupioni silk you can imagine."

The chenille felt great against my skin. It had as good a "hand," as Adrienne said. But the silk . . . "It's a Craftsman-style bungalow. Small rooms, small windows, gorgeous but dark woodwork, and low ceilings. I'm not sure that deep a saturation in the dupioni won't block more light than I'd like."

"How about your buttercream for sheers beneath the silk? That way, you can use the caramel in panels to frame the sheers—you know, leave the drapes open at the sides."

"That could work. I could even fake wider windows that way. What do you have that's sheer in that color range?"

The bolt of gossamer cream stripe Adrienne showed me took my breath away. "Where did you get this?"

Adrienne's smug smile was my only answer.

I rolled my eyes. "Fine. Keep your secrets, but please,

please, please stash away the rest for me, whatever I don't use for Gussie's job. I know I'm going to want more."

"I could do that." Her hazel eyes narrowed. "But it'll cost you."

"More than the fortune you're charging for it?"

"Give me a break, Haley. Where else are you going to find that quality Thai silk for that puny little price?"

I shrugged. "Hey, remember who taught me to bargain—queens of haggle don't do things by halves."

"Marge and I should have known way back then that sooner or later you'd turn our lessons on us."

"And you're loving every minute of it. You'd ream me out if I ponied up whatever you asked without a whimper."

"True, but as your auntie Adie, I reserve the right to refuse to haggle—and to tease."

"Fine. But you better not sell an inch of this silk to anyone else."

"As long as you tell me everything you learn about Marge's killer. And as long as you watch your back. Marge got in someone's way, and I doubt they'll let you find them out. You're a very convenient scapegoat."

"Tell me about it." I sighed. "I'd better get going. I have fences to mend, and I shouldn't put it off. If you'll have one of your minions snip me full-yard samples of the chenille and the silks, plus a satin stripe in creams and caramels or maybe shades of gold for a side chair I want to reupholster. And don't forget the persimmon."

I took another look at my design board. "Oh, I want a floral tapestry with sepia tones for pillows and accessories too. Then I'll be on my way."

"Todd." Adrienne waved over a young man, probably a student at Seattle Pacific University, and gave him precise instructions. But as thorough as she was, the expression on her face told me she had something else on her mind.

When Todd left on his sample safari, I braced myself. "Okay, Adrienne. I'm not leaving until you tell me what's up. Your head's doing about a mile per nanosecond, and I don't think Thai silk calls for that much thought."

She gave me another of her elegant shrugs. "Not here, all right?" She pointed toward her glass-enclosed office.

I nodded. Once we sat, Adrienne behind her beat-up army-surplus-green metal monster of a desk and me on a melt-into-the-clouds leather armchair across from it, she sighed.

"You know I don't like to gossip, but there's something you don't know that might have something to do with all this."

Adrienne had hated the glass-house atmosphere of Hollywood and the notoriety that went with her kind of success. When she fell in love with a Seattle business executive, their dates became a matter of public record. The publicity nearly cost her the love of a wonderful but private man. When Brad proposed, Adrienne turned her back on the bright lights, came home, and produced five mini-Brads.

"If it's something that might keep me out of jail," I said, "please tell me. I don't think that would count as gossip. Last I checked, gossip is idle, self-serving, and malicious. You're none of the above. And you might keep me out of jail, since I did not kill Marge."

Adrienne's smile was forced. "You need to talk to Ozzie."

I gaped. Hadn't I thought the same thing? I scooted my chair closer to the desk and planted my hands on its cold steel top. "What about?"

"He and Marge worked well together, but not always. At least, I know they had an ongoing battle over ownership of the auction house."

"How could they argue about that? The business belongs to—" I winced "—belonged to Marge."

Adrienne reached across the desk and covered my hand with hers. She gave me a gentle smile, then shook her head, her pretty face sad.

"Exactly," she said, "and that was the problem. Ozzie worked for her for almost twenty years. He wanted a piece of the action, a partnership. Minor, yes, but he felt he'd earned the right to part of the profits, not just a salary and commission."

"That could build some resentment. But do you think he'd kill her? He wouldn't have thought he'd inherit the business with that kind of disagreement, don't you think?"

Even though Detective Tsu had shot down my ideas, I hadn't been that far off. Now I wanted someone who'd known both Marge and Ozzie way longer than I had to tell me if she could see the fussy little man as a killer.

Adrienne closed her eyes. She was praying—another one who prayed about everything. They were all around me. I felt more alone than ever now that Marge, the one agnostic I knew, was gone.

"They had a tug-of-war going on," she finally said. "I often wondered if Marge knew something about Ozzie that kept her from moving forward on the partnership, something bad, something he didn't want made public. Otherwise, why object for so long? He made her buckets of money over the years, not only because of all his contacts, but also because of all he sold for her. He's an amazing salesman. I'd have made him a partner."

My eyes nearly popped from their sockets. "You think Marge was capable of blackmail?"

"I wouldn't go that far. I just know something wasn't quite right, and it held her back."

Movement on the other side of the glass wall caught Adrienne's and my attention at the same time. Todd was back, beautiful fabric swatches in hand.

Adrienne stood, relieved, and opened the door. "Well, then. Since you said you had to go, call me and let me know which goods you'll want and how much of each. I can have them delivered to you, at home or at the site, the same day you place the order."

I wasn't about to learn anything more, and Adrienne did need to get back to work. Besides, I had more snooping to do, not to mention those fences I was afraid I'd obliterated. Repair work was called for if I wanted to have a business.

Ozzie Krieger, here I come. Then Noreen . . . and maybe even—did I really have to?—Dutch.

"Thanks for everything," I said, and she understood.

"Be careful, Haley. I . . . I don't know that I can stand to lose you too. I know the Lord says I won't be hit by more than I can bear, but it's already been so much."

I reached up and hugged her hard, fought the tears that stung my eyes, made my voice sound even stronger than usual. "I'll be fine, Adrienne. You'll see. I'm going to be your best customer in no time flat."

"That's my prayer." Tears filled her almond-shaped eyes. "God bless you, sweetie. You're always in my prayers."

For a moment, unaccustomed warmth washed my heart, maybe even a hint of comfort, but then anger rushed back in.

"See ya." I grabbed my samples and fled to my car.

I couldn't think about the emotions Adrienne's prayers had teased awake. I had to focus on the present, on my problems. I had to find out who killed Marge.

Maybe then I'd know what to do with all the rage.

"Is your father home?" I asked Hugh Krieger forty-five minutes later.

The fireplug-shaped man on the roof spit a mouthful of nails into his hand. "Had an appointment with a family. The great-aunt is headed for a nursing home. They asked him to appraise the estate."

"Will the law allow a sale this soon? The auction house is still in probate. Besides, there's a murder investigation going on, and it involves the auction house and everything related to it."

"Murder . . . now there's a topic for ya."

I didn't like his tone of voice, and his poisonous stare wasn't any better. "Yes, one I need to discuss with Ozzie. Do you know what time he'll be home?"

The bullish man looked at the cedar shingle in his hand, then at me. He tossed the wood in the air, as if gauging its heft. He looked down at me again. "I have no idea, but I'm pretty sure he's not interested in your lies."

"What lies? You don't know what I have to discuss with him."

Another toss. "I don't care what you want to talk about. All I know is that Dad's been a wreck since you killed Marge. You think he's going to want to have tea and cookies with you any time soon?"

I sucked in air. No one had talked to me like that, not even Dutch. It nearly brought me to my knees. "I didn't kill Marge, and Ozzie knows that. Did he say I did?"

"No. Dad hasn't talked, but I can read. It's all over the papers. The cops are gonna lock you up any day now."

Not if I could help it. "They have no evidence, no proof, because there is none. I didn't do it."

I took a long shuddering breath, which didn't calm me one bit, but at least my lungs felt as though they might make it another minute or five. "I do need to talk to your father, so please give him the message."

He laughed—not with humor either.

I didn't want to hear another word. "Better yet. Forget I asked. I'll find Ozzie on my own."

Just like I'd have to find Marge's killer.

"Good riddance," Hugh said. "And don't let the door hit ya on the way out."

I didn't look back.

My trusty Honda started right up, thank goodness, and I pulled away, my hands trembling so hard I had trouble holding on to the steering wheel. Funny how one mean-spirited jerk could ruin your day.

Had his father ruined my life?

As I drove away, I didn't know whether to cry or get mad. It didn't look as though I'd solve the puzzle of Marge's murder any time soon, and since both crying and getting mad wasted too much energy, I did neither. I was going to need every ounce of oomph I could beg, borrow, or steal. Well, with all the suspicion coming my way, this wasn't a good time for me to steal anything, not even a nap.

But that was what I wanted. I craved my bed, my down comforter, my dog at my feet, the horror far, far away.

Too bad I'm a grown-up.

That thought flew out the window the moment I pulled into the parking lot at Norwalk's Auction House and saw Dutch drive up from the opposite direction. Why was he here? I wanted him gone. I wanted to yell, bicker, stomp my foot, throw a tantrum. I didn't; I controlled myself. Barely.

We got out of our steel steeds at the same time.

"What are you doing here—"

"What do you think you're doing—"

We stood with legs shoulder-width apart, fists on hips, glaring, disgusted, and not about to budge an inch.

He blinked—figuratively speaking, that is. He rolled his green eyes, then muttered, "You first."

"Okay. What are you doing here?"

"That wasn't what I meant, and you know it. *You* tell *me* what the big idea is. What do you think you'll accomplish here?"

I gave him a smug smile. "Probably the same thing you do."

"I doubt it."

"So why are you here? At least I've helped Marge in the warehouse more times than I can count. And she trusted me enough to leave me the stupid place."

"You know, that smart mouth of yours is probably going to land you in jail faster than any evidence that might show up."

"True, I can talk myself into more trouble than it's worth, but you still haven't told me why you came out here." When he crossed his arms, and his expression grew even more mulish, I figured I'd—again—have to be a grown-up.

"Fine. I'll tell you why I'm here. It's no big deal. I have to talk to Ozzie Krieger, Marge's assistant."

Surprise wiped the stubbornness off his face. "You're still playing Jessica Fletcher Jr. after the disaster at Noreen's?"

"I'm not playing. I came to talk to Ozzie. Is there a law against that?"

"No, but there're plenty against interfering with an ongoing police investigation. And you're doing just that."

Something in my makeup, probably the pastor's kid gene, wouldn't let me lie. "I'm not interfering. I just don't see why I should let someone frame me for killing a woman I love and miss more each day."

"Let the police do their job. Who knows how much evidence is being destroyed just because you've alerted someone. That is, if you're telling the truth and didn't kill the woman."

"I just told you I didn't kill Marge." I'd had enough of the suspicion. I wasn't going to play the game. "Look, Dutch Merrill, I've a question for you. And it's about something I've observed."

"Go ahead. At least I won't kill you if you ask another dumb question. I have nothing to gain by losing you."

"That's what you say. But you're awfully hot on having me

locked up. I wonder why. Did you kill Marge for some weird reason? Is that why you want to pin this on me?"

He dared to laugh. "You know I didn't kill Marge Norwalk. But I'll tell you what. From where I'm standing, you look pretty suspicious. Not only are you totally paranoid, but there's good reason to think you—"

"Haley didn't kill Marge."

We both turned. "Ozzie! I'm so glad to see you. And thanks for telling this wacko the truth."

Ozzie shrugged. "I don't know who killed Marge, but I'm sure it wasn't you."

Dutch took a step forward. "How do you know that?"

The look Ozzie sent me had a truckload of apology in it. "Because, Mr. Merrill, whoever murdered my employer was not only homicidal but also furtive, devoid of conscience, and secretive. Haley Farrell can't keep her mouth shut even if someone staples it for her."

I gaped.

Dutch laughed—again.

Ozzie wrung his hands.

I wanted to scream, but that adult thing held me back. Would Ozzie's less than rousing endorsement stand up in court? After all, he'd exculpated me by insult.

What was up with that?

10

Ozzie's pronouncement seemed to convince Dutch that we were both shy of a load of travertine marble tile. He went to his ratty truck with little more to add than a nasty, "Hope I don't trip over you next place I go."

"Not very polite, huh?"

"Few care for the niceties anymore, Miss Farrell." He looked just like a merry basset hound.

Even while happy, glum.

I was going to have to take the reins in our little chat, but I wasn't sure how to go about it, since I'd been such a smashing success with Noreen and Hugh.

"Ah . . . how about we go inside?" Marge's electric teakettle and espresso machine would give us something to do. Ozzie was a tea aficionado, and Marge had always kept a cartload of choices, both exotic and mundane, at hand. Starbucks, of course, was a staple.

"Very well, miss." He took a key from his pocket and led the way in. But then he tripped.

I followed and sprawled all over the poor man.

"Whtw ohvr mrphw!" he mumbled.

"What did you say?"

"Ufh twdtwu dho whtw ohvr mrphw!"

After a mental checkup of limbs and other stray body parts—they worked—I began to extricate myself from the awkward position. Ozzie didn't help with all the squirming and wriggling he did to try to ditch me off.

"Give me a minute. I'm trying to put my feet on the floor rather than on you." You'd think he'd realize I was looking out for him.

The moment I eased off, Ozzie lurched up. "Why is this steamer trunk in the middle of the hallway? I certainly didn't leave it here this morning when I retrieved an initial-contact information packet for our new clients."

Had my intuition suddenly mushroomed, or was it that obvious that something was rotten in the state of Denmark?

"Why don't you turn on the light?" I asked.

"I tried, Miss Farrell. The switch did not work."

Uh-oh. No power. A trunk in the middle of the hall. Dutch in the vicinity when I got here.

"Do you think someone—"

"Call the authorities, Miss Farrell." Ozzie's voice squeaked, and fear was on his face. "Someone has ransacked the office."

My instincts were getting better.

"I'll get my cell phone. I left it in the car when that slug of a contractor showed up." And like him, it might be gone by now.

But no. It was hiding, as usual, in the farthest reaches of my limitless backpack purse. It took me only seven minutes and fifty-three seconds to snatch it up this time. I shaved four seconds off my previous record.

The dispatcher answered right away. "This is Haley Far-rell," I said, "and I'm at Norwalk's Auction House, and someone broke in here, and there's no power, and there's an antique—it is antique isn't it?"

Ozzie nodded from the doorway, his expression more mournful than before.

I returned to the dispatcher squawking in my ear. "Hang on! I haven't told you everything. There's this antique trunk in the middle of the hall, and Ozzie says it wasn't here when he came by earlier—that was today, wasn't it?"

This nod looked like a woe sundae with a frown on top.

"Yeah, the trunk wasn't in the middle of the hall earlier today. You'd better send someone out here to investigate pretty quick."

Dead silence.

By now I was shivering so hard I almost dropped the phone. "Hey! Are you there? Where'd you go?"

"Are you done babbling?"

"I wasn't babbling. I just wanted to give you all the information."

"Look, lady, how about if you zip it up and let me ask you a couple of questions?"

"Fine." So much for trying to be helpful and thorough. "What do you want to know?"

"To begin with, who are you?"

Nausea hit. "I told you already. I'm Haley Farrell, who're you?"

The guy groaned, and I realized he sounded familiar. "Chris? Christopher Thomas? Is that you?"

"Yes, Haley," my former classmate answered. "It's me. Now how about we do this the right way?"

"Just get someone over here, Chris, would you please? You'd think that just the mention of Marge's name would get some action. She was murdered, you know."

I thought I heard him count to ten. "Yes, Haley, I know Mrs. Norwalk was murdered. And if you'd shut up long enough, I bet you'd hear the siren. Now, are you going to let me do my job?"

He was right. A siren wailed closer and closer. Relief made me shake even more, so I sagged against my Honda, and let the tremors win. "Uh . . . Chris? Do you think I could tell whoever's on their way that stuff you want to know? I feel sorta queasy."

"You still throw up when you get scared?"

The memory of a mammoth spider in my sixth-grade desk didn't help. "Yes, Christopher Dylan Thomas, I still get queasy when I'm nervous, but I don't throw up anymore. And since talking to you does nothing for my stomach, I'll talk to whoever's here."

I closed my clamshell phone with a click.

An unmarked, plain-vanilla sedan pulled in.

I looked over and groaned. I wasn't getting any breaks.

"Hello, Detective Tsu. Sorry to take you away from your desk."

The elegant woman gave me her by now familiar emotionless look. "It's my job."

I was pretty tired of hearing her boast about her job.

A cruiser arrived. I directed the three cops to the door that led to the office side. Ozzie was in the bowels of the building.

Then it dawned on me. He could've trashed all kinds of evidence while I babbled at Chris. "Ah . . . Ms. Tsu?"

"Yes?"

"Mr. Krieger stayed inside while I came out here to report the break-in. I . . . ah . . . wasn't with him all this time, and maybe . . . well . . . he could've—"

"I understand." She strode into the building, her steps surprisingly long for such a petite woman. I felt like a clodhopper giraffe lolloping along in her wake.

After Ozzie and I answered another multitude of questions, the officers pulled out the most impressive kits. They sprinkled black powder over everything, then shone ultraviolet lights on their anything-but-fairy dust. Wherever they found a print, they covered it with what looked like industrial-strength tape, and stored the mess in plastic zipper bags.

I'd only seen this on TV.

Too bad I had such a stake in the investigation. I would have loved to ask these guys all kinds of questions. And even though questions were on today's menu, the only one who got to ask was Detective Tsu.

"And Mr. Merrill drove up at the same time you did. Is that right Ms. Farrell?"

I'd only told her that eleven times. "Yes."

"Could he have been watching for someone to come so that it might appear as if he'd just arrived?"

I grinned. "I like the way you think. The possibility did cross my mind."

"Did you notice anything unusual about him?"

"*He* is unusual. But if you mean did he have dust all over him or was there a cobweb hanging from his nose, then no.

He was no more unusual today than yesterday or the day before."

The graceful eyebrow rose. "You're seeing him?"

"Not like you mean."

"What do you think I mean?"

"Well, I'm not dating the guy, that's for sure. I wouldn't want to." For many reasons, too many to tell the amused Ms. Tsu. "I mean, he's been following me. He has this moronic idea that I killed Marge and sooner or later he's going to catch me doing something that'll give him *the* clue to break the case."

"Moronic, you say?"

"That's what I said. So if the shoe fits the idea, then I guess you can put it on the police's favorite theory too."

The detective chuckled. "You have a way with words."

I bit down on my tongue before it got me in more trouble. Then, when I was sure I wouldn't say anything for which she'd lock me up, I asked, "Anything else?"

Ms. Tsu ran a neatly trimmed, rose-polished nail down the current page on her little notebook. "I don't think so, but you know the drill."

"Sure. You're going to show up when I least expect you with another load of questions—or maybe even the same ones, just worded differently."

This time she smiled. "I'm glad to see we understand each other, Ms. Farrell. Tyler said you were sharp. Glad to see he wasn't too far off the mark."

What was that supposed to mean? But after a comment or two in my recent past about my mouth and its talent for trouble, I just smiled back.

I followed the detective outside. She unlocked her boring car, tossed her elegant black bag onto the passenger seat, and looked up at me. "You know, Ms. Farrell. I don't believe in coincidences."

"What's that supposed to mean?"

"It means," she said, her face expressionless again, "that too many laws have been broken with regards to Marge Norwalk. What's even more curious is that you're a prominent figure in each incident."

"Just because I was at the auction doesn't mean anything. There were 567 other people there too. And if you'll notice, the moment I realized this place was vandalized, I called you guys."

"True. But you have been present both times."

"Do you know where you are? Have you taken a look around you?" I waved toward the surrounding structures. "This isn't your most exclusive neighborhood, you know. Anyone could've broken in."

She glanced at the building next door whose windows were either missing or boarded up. "Come on, Ms. Farrell—"

"Look. You may as well call me Haley, since you're obviously going to be around a whole lot."

"Very well. But you don't really believe some random homeless person broke into the warehouse, do you, Haley?"

I sighed. "No. But it's crazy for you to think I had anything to do with it."

"As I said, I don't believe in coincidences. You were at the auction and found the deceased. You inherited her estate instead of her husband. You were reported as vandalizing a garbage can at the Norwalk residence—"

"I didn't vandalize the trash! Two of the biggest rats on earth were having themselves a feast. They're the ones that . . ."

I'd walked right into her trap. "Okay, fine. I went to talk to Steve, but when I got there I . . . er . . . um . . . found myself in a . . . a . . . predicament."

"So I hear." She chuckled. "That must be why the cat tackled you."

"You didn't see that. You arrived after Bali H'ai ran off—"

"Tell me you didn't name your cat Bali H'ai."

"That monster's not mine! She's Bella's, the neighbor across the street. Besides, you weren't there when it happened."

"The cat's not important, Haley. I went to your home because I'd received a call about your exploits in the garbage shed. I saw an interesting scenario and pulled over to watch. I saw the cat go for you."

"Not one of my finer moments, I'll admit."

"I knew that." She shook her head. "But I also heard you've harassed Noreen Daventry and Hugh Krieger since the garbage incident."

I went to object, but she held me off with an upraised slender finger. "Hear me out, please. Now I respond to a call about a break-in, and I find you in the thick of it. You must admit, I have good reason for my suspicion."

"If that's the best you can do to try to pin this on me, then I hope you haven't missed the boat with Dutch Merrill."

"What do you mean?"

"Well, unless you're pretending ignorance, I'm sure you've noticed he's been right behind me every one of those times. Except maybe at the slimy lawyer's office and on

Marge's will. But every other time you mentioned, Dutch was there."

"And . . . ?"

"And unless he was doing it for the sole purpose of driving me stark raving mad, then maybe there's a good reason why he showed up at all those suspicious events. Suspicious to you, that is."

"I don't see why you would suspect Mr. Merrill."

"Then you should also not see any reason to suspect me, if your logic's going to hold water." I had a thought. "Have you fingerprinted Dutch? I wonder if you'd hit a match with what you guys got here today."

She sat behind the wheel and slammed the door shut. "I have fingerprinted Mr. Merrill, but I hadn't thought to see if any of today's prints match his. I don't see that he had any motive for killing Marge Norwalk, much less the opportunity to do so. He and Noreen, together with about nine other auction-goers, alibi each other quite well."

I smiled in triumph. "Guess what? I sat with them the entire morning. So that clears me too. Go follow someone else, please. Let me get my business and my life on track."

The car purred to life. "I'm sorry, Haley, but you don't have an alibi for the most crucial time. The people you mentioned saw you get up moments after Marge left the room. They can't place you again until they ran to the scene of the crime. That's where everyone agrees they saw you next."

As surely as it had happened to me years before, my throat closed, this time from fear of what might be, whereas that time it had from the reality of what was. Once again, someone held all the power. Once again, I was a victim.

I had barely lived through the first attack; I didn't know if I would survive the second.

"You don't have to stay and clean up this mess, Miss Farrell," Ozzie said. "I can certainly do it myself."

Sure, and in the meantime, pitch anything incriminating. "That's fine, Ozzie. Since it looks as though I'll have to deal with all of this one day, I'd just as soon get started now."

His sad face tightened into anger, and his lips sprouted a white rim. "Very well, miss. Please do let me know if I can be of assistance."

What was his deal? Hadn't he realized even the twentieth century was done and gone? He reminded me of a Victorian butler in a black-and-white classic movie.

"Thanks, Ozzie."

It didn't take long to realize that whatever the person who tossed the place wanted, they thought they'd find it among Marge's papers. A blanket of sales records hid the mahogany desk and cordovan leather executive chair. Because of the chaos, it was going to take time to sort through the mess and familiarize myself with Marge's filing system.

I started a series of piles. Receipts went into one, estate inventories into another, a year's worth of appraisals into the next. The rest wound up on the miscellaneous pile. This one grew at an alarming rate.

I picked up what looked like a memo, but a phrase caught my eye. *"It is exceedingly mean-spirited of you to continue to deny me the opportunity to advance. To leave and seek employment elsewhere at this stage in my life would be sheer folly, as you well know.*

"Forgiveness is a virtue, and while you assure me you've given it, your actions appear far more those of an extortionist extracting yet another drop of blood from her victim.

"I have more than paid restitution for my transgression, and you have even said you understood the desperation that drove me to it, yet you still seem to relish withholding the opportunity, the right, that would otherwise be mine. I don't know how much longer I can bear the status quo. Every man has a breaking point, and I'm afraid mine is frighteningly close. I dread to think what might push me over the edge, and much more what I might do once that happens."

The thinly veiled threat was signed by Ozzie.

And I was alone with him in this huge, empty warehouse. Not good.

I folded the memo, stuffed it into the zippered side pouch of my backpack purse, and then ran back into the hallway. "On second thought, Ozzie," I called, my voice reedy and shaky, "I'm heading home now. I'll wait until the power's back. The window in Marge's office doesn't let in as much light as I thought at first. See ya!"

Ozzie did have a motive for murder. And although I spent a few minutes with him during the intermission, most of the time I was on my own.

Who knows what he did while I was gone.

Some days just don't end soon enough. Today was one of them.

I went to the *dojo* to clear my head of all the crud, but when I got there, I walked right into Tyler's setup. While I'd never seen Detective Tsu in any of my classes—until the one she taught, that is—tonight she stood front and center among the other students.

I felt like screaming and yelling and crying and kicking—not a very adult thing. That was how I felt but not what I did. I bowed before Tyler with all the respect he was due as my *sensei*, and not once did I pout . . . much.

Even when he chuckled at my discomfort.

Even though I found no humor in the situation.

Really, I didn't.

I focused like a good little judo student and did everything he asked the class to do. In fact, I did so well that I managed to forget he and the omnipresent Ms. Tsu were anywhere near.

Until Master Tyler decided this was the night for sparring.

When he told me to greet my partner, I learned the true meaning of the cliché about looks that could kill. The one I shot could've felled a bull three counties away. It didn't do a thing to him.

Ms. Tsu and I took our places in the center of the room. I don't know if the rest of our classmates could sense the tension between us, but the air seemed to bristle with something tight, something that challenged me for every breath I took.

I met Ms. Tsu's hazel gaze and, without looking away, I bowed.

She did the same.

We'd both thrown an invisible gauntlet. Everyone knew it. Even Tyler, the wretch.

We slowly, warily circled each other. I riveted my attention on my opponent. More than a sparring match was taking place.

I felt as though my future was at stake.

Step . . . sidestep . . . another one. Ms. Tsu's graceful movements might have lulled me into a sense of superiority; I was taller, more muscular. But this wasn't that kind of a match. Martial arts are about the mind, understanding human nature, thinking ahead of the other person's next move.

She made her move.

I anticipated and blocked it.

We resumed our circling motion, silent, focused, determined.

With Tyler's lessons in mind, I paid attention to the detective's breathing, even the rhythm of the opening and closing of her eyelids. After eons of this, I waited for the moment when her lids dropped a fraction slower than before. Then I lunged.

She parried.

I backed away.

The tension grew.

My heartbeat sped, but I made my breathing even, measured, controlled. I couldn't let fear get in my way. I couldn't let her psych me out.

She attacked.

I thwarted her.

I pounced.

She repelled me.

Sweat beaded my forehead. A drop rolled by millimeters down my spine. I took note and let the sensation pass. I had to focus on the detective, the woman whose efforts would either clear me or condemn me to an unthinkable future.

The dangerous dance went on for what felt like hours. I

had no notion of time, no sense that anyone else existed. My world had shrunk to encompass only a cop and me.

Tyler finally brought things to an end. "Enough! It's ten fifteen and way past my bedtime."

I blinked.

Ms. Tsu shuddered.

We both faced Tyler.

"Go on. Bow, then head to the shower. Everyone left about forty-five minutes ago."

I looked around. The three of us stood alone in the large room. I hadn't noticed anything, anything but Detective Tsu.

Cold suddenly overtook me. I shivered, then faced my foe and bowed. "Thank you."

She bowed as well. "You're a worthy opponent."

Tyler snorted. "I wish you'd both just knock it off already. Lila, she didn't kill Marge. And you, Haley, had better get that cop chip off your shoulder. Lila had nothing to do with what happened four years ago."

I gasped. "How . . . how could you?"

"I can because I've watched you, and I know you better than you think. I also know Lila, and I know Marge's killer won't go free. Not like—"

"Don't," I said through clenched teeth. "Don't even say it. As long as she's working so hard to prove I killed Marge, I'll reserve the right to doubt."

My attacker was given a brief probation and forty hours of community service, thanks to the Mickey-Mouse investigation the police conducted. Is it any wonder that I couldn't make myself trust homicide detective Lila Tsu?

11

Little by little my world had started to peel apart. I'd worked so hard to overcome the devastation of four years ago, and now I felt as if I was being shoved right back into the pit.

This time I didn't have Mom or Marge, and Dad spoke only of God, that God who let the chaos happen in the first place.

I left the practice room with what dignity I could muster, went to the locker room for my duffel bag, and left the *dojo* as fast as I could. The drive home was an exquisite form of torture. Painful memories tangled with rioting emotions.

The idea that one person could wield power over another, enough to ruin or take a life, seemed contrary to all I'd learned in Sunday school about a loving, generous God. Now I was stuck in a hole of someone else's digging, unable to catch a foothold and pull myself out. How could I square that with a benign God? How loving could he be if he abandoned the children he called his own to such a rotten fate?

I didn't see it.

I loved Midas. I'd never leave him so that someone more powerful could abuse or destroy him. I'd protect him with all I had.

If God was all-powerful, why did he abandon me? Why did he abandon Marge? Why did he continue to leave me at the mercy of merciless vultures?

As I drove up the manse's driveway, I knew I had to pull myself together. I was headed down a familiar, frightening road. I'd already traveled that nightmare, and I couldn't do it again. I couldn't drag Dad down it either. The first time had been almost more than he could bear.

I'd seen in him the pain of a father whose child had been harmed. I'd have to put on a happy face. I'd have to smile and kid around, at least until I could escape to the freedom of my room.

But exhaustion claimed me. I felt beaten, tired, drained; I wondered how I could pull off any charade. From the recesses of my memory, those dust-bunnied corners I avoided like the plague, my mother's voice whispered, *"He'll never leave you nor forsake you."*

Hunger gnawed at me, and it had nothing to do with the dinner I'd missed. It was hunger for the assurance I'd once had in God's provision, the assurance that he'd be there to catch me if I fell.

At the same time, I felt as if I'd plummeted down a black void where every inch I traveled, new and riskier traps reached out to snag me. I was so alone.

Midas's exuberant barks pierced my desperation. I couldn't stay in the car all night. Sooner or later Dad would worry enough to come for me, and I couldn't let him see how far I'd relapsed.

I took a soul-deep breath and opened the Honda's door. Once inside, I fended off my dog's ecstatic welcome. "It's not as if you hadn't seen me for years, you big goof!"

The best thing about a dog is that no matter what, he always welcomes you home. Tonight, Midas helped me mask my dismal mental state.

"Did you have a good class?" Dad asked from behind his newspaper.

Swell. "Ah . . . the usual. We worked on strength moves, and then Tyler had us spar."

"How'd you do?"

How did I do? Not well. "He called it a draw. Neither one of us would concede the match, and we'd already gone an hour and a half past the end of the lesson."

"It did seem late. With all that's happened lately, I wondered if I'd have to call that lovely lady detective to see if she could find you."

Hah! If he only knew. "I'm fine, Dad, but the lesson wiped me out, so I'm off to bed." I dropped a kiss on his balding head, and before he had a chance to get a good look at me, I ran upstairs.

"Good night, dear." I heard him rummage through the sections of the newspaper, and then the TV went on. Good. His news program would keep him busy until I fell asleep.

I dragged myself through a lick-and-a-promise bedtime wash and was about to crawl into bed when Dad's yell jolted me to army-recruit attention. "What's up?"

"You'd better hurry down here and listen to this. I'm not sure what it might mean for you."

Dad was no alarmist. That much worry made me run.

"It would seem," the newscaster's resonant voice boomed out, "that murder's tentacles spread farther than most would think. A source under promise of anonymity tells us that socialite Noreen Daventry is involved, indirectly perhaps, in the murder of local businesswoman Marge Norwalk. At first, authorities discarded her as a potential suspect, but word of an affair with the deceased's husband has made the investigators take a second look."

"Is that true?" Dad asked, his voice quiet, distressed.

"That the cops are looking at Steve and Noreen?"

"No. That Steven committed adultery with that woman."

I had no patience with deception in general and sexual sin in particular, but Dad saw things in an eternal light. "I saw them together the other day. It was disgusting, especially since Marge had only been dead a couple of days."

"So he'd been unfaithful to her."

"It would seem so."

"Your mother was afraid of that."

"I remember, Dad. You agreed."

He shook his head, sadness on his face. "It's beyond me how people can hurt others so easily."

It wasn't beyond me. I knew all about it. But before I had to respond, the commercial was over, and the news anchor was back.

"Another element in this case," he said, "is the widower's sudden unemployment. A teacher at the Carleton-Higgins Academy in Wilmont, Mr. Steven Norwalk, was relieved of his duties when the headmaster learned of the math teacher's romantic escapades. It seems he figured in a recent messy divorce, and students have linked him to one teacher and at least one former student. Now there are questions about the widower's innocence. And if he had something to do with his wife's death, was Mrs. Daventry involved too?"

My stomach churned. I couldn't listen to another word. I stood. "Sorry, Dad. I can't sit through any more. Gotta go."

This time I burrowed under my blanket, and Midas took up his spot at my feet. Nothing would get me out of my cocoon before daylight. Sleep was no longer a possibility.

I had too much burning up the synapses in my mind.

Saturday morning dawned clear and warm. Unfortunately, a phone call dragged me awake a brief hour and forty-five minutes after the last time I'd checked the clock.

"H'lo?"

"Haley, honey," Gussie said, her voice strained and full of apology. "I'm so sorry to do this to you, but I'm afraid I can't get out of bed this morning. Tom is preparing my morphine pump, and you know how that knocks me out. I won't be able to help you with today's meeting."

Great. I'd forgotten that the second episode of "Haley Trashes the Missionary Society" was slated for this morning. And now I wouldn't have Gussie to count on. But what could I say?

I sat up. "Don't worry about it. I'll figure out some way to get through it without making too much of a mess of things."

"Give yourself some credit, dear. I know that if you set your mind to it, you'll succeed. You have enormous energy and far more talent than any of the rest of us. Use your gifts wisely, and the Lord will see you through."

Yeah, sure. "Ah . . . I'll call you after we're done to see how you feel and to bring you up to date on what the ladies decide."

"You might wind up talking with Tom, you know. I'll sleep on and off for the rest of the day."

"That's fine. He can tell me how you're doing, and I can tell him what kind of hash I made of things."

"Stop that, Haley," Gussie scolded gently. "You can do far better than you give yourself credit for. Now head on out, and don't let Penny steamroller you."

Boy, did I ever do a great job of reassuring the woman. "Don't mind me, Gussie. I just made some lousy jokes. I'll be fine—the missionary society will be fine. You'll see. You just take care, and get the rest you need."

After I hung up, Midas came and nosed his way into an ear scratching. "Yep, big guy, I sure do have talent, don't I?"

But time wasn't on my side, so I threw on a long denim skirt and an embroidered cotton blouse and reined my hair into a braid. Birkenstocks in hand, I flew through the kitchen.

"I'm on my way to a missionary society meeting, Dad. If I'm not back by twelve thirty, send out the troops. Penny'll probably have fed me to cannibals somewhere in the deepest heart of . . . of . . . well, I don't know where, but you get my drift."

Dad just shook his head, his attention on the batter in his tub-sized yellowware mixing bowl.

I darted into the meeting room just as the light on the coffee urn turned red. I smiled at Ina. "Bliss is forthcoming."

"I remembered you like the Starbucks House Blend." She

patted a five-pound sack of my favorite source of caffeine. "Let me know if it's too weak."

I helped myself to a brimming mugful. I closed my eyes to savor the aroma and the taste in my mouth. "It's perfect, Ina, thanks. But you didn't have to go to that much trouble just for me. I'll drink any coffee, especially in the morning."

"I know that, but your father's told me and Sandy how much you like this particular kind. It's only a few pennies more per pound than the regular grocery-store stuff, and it does seem to wake one up a bit faster."

Yay for a quicker return to full function!

Although I bumbled my way through the meeting, by the time I adjourned it, the society was still intact and I hadn't throttled Penny. The temptation had hit more than once though.

I'd begun to gather the folders of fundraiser info that Sarah Osborn had put together, when the hiss of gossip came from my right.

"Did you catch last night's late news?" Penny asked.

I looked over to see whose ear she was bending. I should've known. Carla Stewart was the town's human repository of rumor and innuendo, and outright slander and gossip too.

Carla nodded. "Who could've missed you-know-who's merry widower splashed all over the place?"

"Well," Penny answered, "we all warned Marge about that gold-digger pretty boy, but she wanted the guy enough to marry him, no matter what anyone told her."

I should have said something to stop them, but I hated to miss anything that could help.

"Noreen gave Steve an ultimatum," Carla said.

Penny shrugged. "Sure. She told him it was either divorce court or the road for him. But he was in no hurry to dump Marge."

"Why would he be?" Carla countered. "My niece knows Noreen's housekeeper's daughter, and she says Noreen wasn't going to share her millions with Steve. She'd had her lawyer do one of those prenups, and he was only getting an allowance once they married."

Penny tsk-tsked. "That would crimp his style. Marge spoiled him with the goodies her money bought."

"A gold digger never falls in love with anyone but himself," Carla added. "Besides the other fool's money, that is."

"Oh, Steve isn't in love with Noreen any more than he was with Marge." Penny chuckled. The sound grated on my ears. "My dentist is the one who did Steve's caps, and she says he complained plenty about Noreen. He said she was fun for ... well, for kicks, if you get what I mean, but he also said more than once that he'd never tie himself to that shark in any way, shape, form, or fashion. And Dr. Worley says that's how he said it too."

Carla pursed her purple-lipsticked mouth. "I believe it."

I'd had all I could stomach. I fixed them both with my sternest glare. "I think you should think before you spread that kind of thing. Gossip's nasty, and it reflects back on those who pass it on. Besides, Marge hasn't been dead long, and look at the kind of stuff you're saying about her. Let her at least rest in peace for a few days."

Penny gave me one of her poisonous looks. "Marge wasn't much better herself."

My temper did a rapid boil. "Watch what you say about a woman who can't defend herself anymore."

"She couldn't have defended herself," Penny shot back. "She didn't have the gall to complain about that gigolo she married, not without coming across as the biggest hypocrite of all time."

She'd gone too far. "How can you say that? Marge was no hypocrite."

"Maybe," Penny conceded, "but she would've been if she'd complained about her husband's flings. She had no room to talk."

I couldn't believe what I was hearing. "Are you accusing Marge of adultery?"

Penny smiled her smarmy, pompous grimace and crossed her arms. "She was what she was."

I didn't know what to say. I'd never known Marge to be anything but devoted to Steve, and I said so to Penny.

"Oh no," she answered. "Marge didn't cheat on Steve, at least not that I know—"

"Me neither," Carla cut in.

I frowned. "Then why . . . ?"

"You knew her now," Penny said with an expansive gesture. "It was a while back when she was up to her tricks. For a while there, it seemed there wasn't an adult male in Wilmont who she hadn't . . . shall we say, sampled?"

Carla chuckled. "Some women even started to drive their husbands to work, and then they'd pick them up in the evening. That way they were sure the men weren't going off with Marge."

"That's crazy," I said. "You're so off base—"

"Carla might have exaggerated a bit," Penny said, "but Marge had a terrible reputation. No one understood why your sainted mother wanted to have anything to do with the woman."

I shook my head in disbelief.

"Haley," Bella said, her hand on my forearm. "It's pretty hard to hear bad stuff about people you love, but Marge did some crummy things back then. I never understood why she messed around with married men, but that's the truth."

"But—"

"That doesn't mean you shouldn't have loved her," Bella added. "And it doesn't give these two snakes the right to go smarmy just days after the woman died."

"Give me a break, Bella." Penny huffed and puffed a bit, then said, "You probably did the same, back when you looked better than what passes for high-priced models these days."

Bella snorted. "Thanks for the weird compliment, but I don't paint myself holier than thou like you two. Marge had flaws. We all do. Christ's the perfect one, and God forgives us thanks to him."

"Amen," Ina said, joining the conversation. "And what you two were just doing is just as sinful, in its way, as what Marge did."

Carla narrowed her brown eyes. "Fine. If you feel better calling me a sinner, then fine. But I'll have you know that Marge was up to her old stuff again."

"No, she wasn't!" I cried before I could stop myself.

"Sure, she was," Carla argued. "My niece said Marge

was getting phone calls from some man at weird hours, times when Steve wasn't around or else had gone to sleep. Always the same man. And I'll have you know Marge's housekeeper is my baby sister, Molly. So you can trust everything I say."

"That's it," I said. "I've had it. And besides, I adjourned this meeting a while back. You'd all better go home. That's where I'm going. I can't stand any more slander from anyone else."

Bella ran up as I reached the door. "I'm sorry, Haley. I wouldn't have said anything about it. They're sort of right. At least, they're right about Marge's past. It's gonna be hard for you to accept, but at least people do change when they get older. We do—sometimes—grow wiser."

I sighed. "Thanks, Bella. I'll keep that in mind."

I did. So much so that I couldn't think of much besides Marge, the allegations of promiscuity, and Noreen and Steve.

Had either of them killed Marge?

If Steve wasn't willing to give up Marge's generosity, he might have been driven to murder if Marge found out about the affair and threatened to kick him out. At the same time, Noreen might have wanted Steve so much, an obsessive thing, that jealousy might have driven her to kill her rival.

On my way back to the manse, I remembered the woman with the endless patience for a wounded soul. Marge hadn't been the religious kind like Penny and Carla, but I'd always thought she was a good person. Now, in the last two days, I'd learned things about her that made me wonder about my mentor. There was that business with Ozzie, and now all this stuff about adultery too.

Who had Marge really been? And was that what I had to know to find out who'd killed her?

Who knew?

Not me. I only knew that the more I tried to learn about the woman I'd admired, the less I seemed to know her. And the more questions I had. Was I going to have any answers before it was too late? Before Detective Tsu locked me up?

I felt iced, numb, scared.

Only time would tell.

Later that evening I followed through on my promise to check up on Gussie. But rather than telephone, I decided to drive over. Even if she was still too medicated for a visitor, I could at least keep Tom company for a while. He always seemed lost when Gussie wasn't around.

He opened the door at my first ring. "Haley! Gussie said you might call to see how she was doing, but this is unexpected."

"I figured you could put up with me for a bit even if she was too sleepy for a visitor."

"Well, of course I can." He stepped aside. "Come on in."

Even though his words were welcoming, something about the way he wouldn't meet my gaze told me things weren't kosher with him. Once I stood in the living room I was re-decorating, I faced him.

"What's wrong, Tom? Is it Gussie? Is she worse? Is there anything I can do to help?"

He turned away. "You're right. Gussie's not well, not a lot better than this morning. But that's pretty typical. When these flare-ups hit, it takes her days to get over them."

I watched him fold the day's newspaper into precise rectangles. Then he slipped the bundle into a rack that already had its share of newsprint, and then some. But when he folded the quilted throw Gussie used on her legs to keep away even the hint of a chill, I'd had enough.

"What is it, Tom? Please tell me."

When he faced me, I realized he looked awful. His words confirmed that he felt as bad as he looked.

"Detective Tsu stopped by earlier today. She had a number of questions for me, and I hated to answer them."

That sick feeling in the pit of my stomach took hold of me again. "Why is that? What did she want to know?"

Tom fisted his hands at his sides. "She wanted to know what I saw the day of the auction."

My flaky stomach was up to its tricks again. I wondered if I'd make it to the toilet if it turned itself inside out. Still, I had to know what had upset this kind man.

"What did you tell her?"

He took a deep breath, and only then did he look me in the eye. "I told her I saw you leave the parlor right after Marge did, and that not long after that I saw you behind the house, near the portable toilets, close to where you found Marge."

I gasped but couldn't talk.

Tom went on. "She wanted to know if I ever saw you again—before you screamed for help when you found Marge's body, that is."

"Wha . . . what did you tell her?"

"I couldn't lie, Haley. I had to tell her I didn't see you again. Not until I saw you on the ground by Marge's body. I had to tell her you were holding the rock she says killed Marge."

12

How do I always wind up in this kind of mess? Here, the man tells me he's practically sealed my fate—a lousy one—and I have to reassure him that he's done the right thing, that I don't hold it against him.

Truth is, I don't. How's that for insane?

"Don't let it upset you so much, Tom," I said for about the zillionth time. "I did leave the parlor right after Marge announced the intermission, and I left because I had to use the toilet. You did see me back there by the port-a-potties."

"But the policewoman seemed to think that proved you killed Marge."

"She's been trying to prove it from the start. I didn't do it, and I'm just going to have to show her."

How? I didn't have a clue.

A clue? You bet I didn't—have one, that is. Was I in trouble or what?

I went on. "That's up to me, you know. You did the right thing. You had to tell the truth. Someone else will have to do the same and remember me at the catering tent. In fact, I should find the guy who sliced my turkey and the girl who served my pasta salad. They'll remember me."

Tom smiled, with way too much relief. "Oh yes! Of course," he said. "I'm sure you'll jog their memories. You're a memorable young woman. I feel so much better now. I couldn't live with the knowledge that I'd consigned you to jail just because you went to the bathroom."

Yep, that'd be me, all right. The woman convicted of peeing at the wrong time.

A hysterical giggle burst out, and Tom took that to mean that I was just peachy dandy.

"I'm so glad to see how well you take even this kind of thing. It's a tribute to your parents and the faith they shared with you. No wonder Gussie loves you so much. You're an outstanding young Christian, Haley."

I wasn't. Anything but, really, but I couldn't explain it to Tom. Besides, panic rumbled in my gut, and I knew I had to run.

"Ah . . . well, thanks for the compliment, and it's too bad that Gussie's not better yet. I'll call her tomorrow . . . see how she's doing. Give her my love."

With the brass doorknob in my hand, I felt a hair better. "Gotta go." I shot him a grimace that posed as a smile, then ran as if the hounds of hell were nipping at my heels.

Well, if you asked Dad, my apostasy was a lot like that kind of chase. He'd said any number of times that no matter how fast and how long I ran, God wouldn't give up on me. From where I stood—or ran—he'd given up four years ago. The hounds of hell? I wasn't sure about them. I figured if God could dump me, then somewhere along the line all the horror that seemed determined to catch up and devour me would sooner or later give up too.

I hoped.

When I got home, I found a note from Dad on the kitchen table. He'd gone for a lecture at Seattle Pacific University, some theologian from England or Scotland or somewhere abroad. He'd talked about it for a couple of days.

Good. I wouldn't have to dance around the trouble I was in. I didn't want to tell my father any more half truths or babble gobbledygook at him. I just wanted to camp out in my room and not show my face again until someone fixed everything that was so screwed up.

Since that wasn't about to happen any time soon, I went to sleep instead.

I didn't have anything to do the next day. My Sundays were usually quiet and peaceful, especially since Dad spent most of the day at church. It was his busiest day. I needed time alone to think things through, maybe even piece together some of the chunks of the puzzle of Marge's death.

But that's not what I got.

At nine thirty, well after Dad left for the morning's first service—he did two each Sunday—the doorbell rang. Midas, of course, went nuts.

"Give me a break." I threw on a ratty old terry-cloth robe. "Don't people sleep or go to church anymore?"

I opened the door and had my answer. Detective Tsu and a couple of her giant Smurfs stood there, more grim faced than I'd ever seen them.

"This doesn't look good," I said.

Detective Tsu shook her head. Her smooth hairstyle made me reach up for my wild mop. Any effort to control my hair was wasted; the stuff flew out in all directions, headed off where no woman's hair had gone before.

"I left the parlor at the beginning of the intermission," I said to stem the interrogation I knew was coming, "and I did go to the port-a-potty. Then I went to the catering tent, asked the big bald guy to slice some turkey breast for me, and had the blond girl serve me pasta. I sat at a corner table—by myself—to eat. Then I headed back to the house, and Ozzie Krieger ran up to me. He asked me to help him look for Marge, and you know the rest."

The detective's lips were tight, and her nostrils flared ever so slightly. "Ms. Farrell—"

"You know all this, because I gave you guys this same statement that afternoon, and I've answered questions about my whereabouts around a dozen times already. My answers are the same, since that's exactly what I did. According to the TV, you guys are big on consistent answers. How's that for consistency?"

"It's fine, but that's not why we're here."

"Oh." Her expression sent me reeling back into that black hole I knew so well. "I really don't want to know why you're here, then, but I've a feeling you're going to tell me anyway."

Something softened the look she gave me. "I'm afraid I am." She slipped a hand into her ultrachic purse and withdrew a couple of sheets of paper. Her hazel eyes met mine. She swallowed, and her smooth throat rippled.

I leaned against the door frame for support. A black cloud congealed at the edge of my awareness.

"This is a warrant for your arrest, Ms. Farrell. You have to come with us to the station."

Darkness rushed in. I fought against it. I couldn't let it win. Not this time. I scrabbled for logical thought, some perspective, but it didn't come. I floundered in my thoughts; desperation seized me. My warm, cozy bed sang a siren song, but there'd be no escape this time.

Shudders shook me. I forced my eyes open, but my vision blurred. The urge to scream overtook me, but I refused to indulge it. "I didn't do it." My voice came out in a croak. My throat tightened; my lungs strained for air. "You have to find out who did. Don't let them get away with it."

Proclaiming my innocence did no good. I'd been blaring it to anyone I got to listen right from the get-go. This time I said it for myself. I couldn't lose sight of reality no matter how surreal things got.

Detective Tsu nodded to one of her officers. He stepped forward, a pair of handcuffs in hand.

Bile seared my throat. I gagged. "Do . . . do you really have to do that? I'll go to the car with you." My teeth chattered so hard I almost couldn't speak. "Sooner or later . . . later now . . . you'll figure out who killed Marge. I get nothing out of resisting you."

"It's police procedure," Detective Tsu said. "I'm sorry."

"Are you really?" I shouldn't have said it, but she'd made me crazy from the moment I met her. My hands clenched; the skin on my knuckles turned white. "I would think, since you've been so determined to prove me guilty, that you'd be jumping up for joy right now."

"I regret the opinion you've formed of me." Although her

speech was squeaky proper and I'd never heard her use any real slang, this statement came with a bucketful of starch.

She went on. "I put this off as long as I could, but after a witness not only placed you in the vicinity of the murder but also saw your hand on the murder weapon, it became difficult to explain my delay. My minor doubt as to your guilt does nothing to counter those fingerprints and your inheritance. My chief would never understand a draw in a sparring match, much less a martial arts instructor's tribute."

So Tyler's words had counted for something.

"You do know I passed out when I found Marge," I said. "I fell, and that's probably when my hand landed on that miserable rock."

"Your hand wasn't laying on the rock, Ms. Farrell. Two witnesses confirm this. You held that bloody rock in your hand, tight. That's why we found your prints all over it."

I sucked in air. My hands hurt, and I concentrated on unfurling each finger. My nails left crescent marks on my palms. "Who besides Tom Stoker could say that?"

Detective Tsu shrugged. "It can't hurt to tell you that Dutch Merrill said the same thing that afternoon. He hasn't changed his story yet."

That miserable cheat. Again.

A ripping surge of anger grabbed me, and I welcomed it. "Didn't I tell you he's everywhere I go? He even found me. Don't you think he could've stuffed the rock in my hand when he got there?"

"That's a bit far-fetched." Ms. Tsu looked at me from head to toe. "Don't you want to get dressed?"

I remembered my ancient robe. "Do the Smurfs have to keep me company while I do?"

She smiled. "No. One will take the side of the house where your room's located, and I'll stand by your door until you're ready. It's police procedure, even though I doubt you'll try to run. You seem to prefer to meet challenges head-on."

To my surprise, that last comment came with a drop of admiration. I didn't know how much truth there was to her assumption, but I wasn't about to change her opinion. It might count for something down the road.

"You're right. I'll fight this all the way." There was one more thing. "I have a favor to ask. My dad's not very young, and we lost my mother about a year ago now. He took it hard." So did I, but that had no place in this mess, aside from the ravening loneliness her loss left behind. "He was also a good friend to Marge. I . . . I'd rather he didn't have to see me handcuffed, and I'd also prefer to tell him what's about to happen."

I swallowed hard, tried to swallow the lump from my throat. Nothing happened, so I blinked against the tears. "I couldn't stand it if he walked out of church and saw you drag me away. And I don't want him to hear about it from a parishioner, see it on the news, or read it in the paper."

"I do understand, Haley."

The warmth in Detective Tsu's voice almost did me in. I nodded and went upstairs. She didn't follow, and I appreciated what that said. I did, though, check outside my window. One of her Smurfs paced up and down the yard on that side of the house.

I sighed. How did one dress for jail? That had to rank right up there as the number one advice no fashionista ever gave.

Certain that whatever I wore would be taken away, I rooted around my dresser for comfortable clothes. A soft, long cotton skirt and a white T-shirt seemed best—not too ratty, in case some stupid photographer decided to snap a shot of the accused killer, but not too funky or dressy either.

Again hysteria threatened. An inappropriate giggle slipped out. At the same time, the tears I'd fought downstairs ran down my cheeks and into the corners of my mouth. A sob wracked me. I didn't think I'd make it through the next minute, much less the rest of the day.

I reached for the anger that had seen me through so much, the anger that just minutes ago had surfaced at the thought of Dutch, but it seemed to have skittered just beyond my grasp. I had to do something. I wasn't going to just roll over and give in. Then the church bells rang.

Dad. I had to be strong for him. He'd been strong for me before, and this would devastate him just as much.

I looked at my parents' portrait on the dresser. They'd had it taken on their silver anniversary, three years ago. I could do it. They'd taught me to be strong, to weather anything and everything. For Dad's sake and Mom's memory, I'd see this through.

Marge's killer would not get away with it.

I went downstairs. "I'm ready."

Detective Tsu turned from the curio cabinet where Mom's collection of eastern European Easter eggs took center stage. "These are lovely. Are they yours?"

"They are now, but my mother's the one who collected them."

"They represent hope, you know."

I sucked in a breath. Unless I was much mistaken, the über-professional, ultraserious Detective Tsu had just sent me a message. Did she really think that somehow, some way, at some unknown time in the future, I'd see the dawn of hope? Did she know something she had yet to tell me?

Did she see an Easter at the end of my darkness?

Time flew by in a blur of misery. Telling Dad that I was headed to jail stood as the second worst moment of my life, the worst being the attack four years ago. It was even worse than Mom's passing, since she'd been in so much pain before she went.

"I'll be praying, honey," was all he said, but the grief in his eyes and the slump of his shoulders spoke more than any puny words could say.

I didn't cry until I sat in the cruiser. Then Detective Tsu sat at my side. "I really am sorry, and I've never said this to a prisoner."

My tears gave her an E.T.-ish alien look, kind of drippy and bleary. I sniffled before I tried to form words. "I have to ask. Are you sorry you arrested me because you know I'm not guilty, or are you sorry you arrested me because you're sure I did it and wish I hadn't?"

"I'm not sure I know the answer yet."

"Then what do you have to be sorry for?"

"That I've had to arrest a woman I'm starting to like."

That set me back. "I don't know what to say."

"Don't say anything. Just hope that if, as you say, you are innocent, the truth will soon turn up."

"I've been on that kick from the start. That's why you kept

tripping over me, so to speak—No! You're not the one who said that. Dutch Merrill said it."

"He really has been everywhere you have, hasn't he?"

"Makes a girl wonder what his stake is in all this, doesn't it?

"Hmm . . ."

"Okay. You don't have to answer, but at least listen to me." I figured she was stuck with me for another fifteen minutes, barring any church-rush traffic jam, if such a thing existed, so it didn't hurt to try to get a reaction from her.

Well, I could try, anyway. The woman was as readable as a treatise on the mating habits of mutant gnats.

"Look. If you think I look guilty because I've been in the wrong place at the wrong time, then Dutch should look just as guilty, right?"

She shrugged.

I went on despite her apathetic response. "I hate rumors, okay? But before the auction, when Marge first told me she'd recommend me to Noreen, she also said she'd heard Noreen was involved—personally, that is—with some builder. I didn't expect it to be Dutch, but who else would it be?"

"I heard something like that."

"So here's my question. What was Noreen really up to? We know she was messing around with Steve, but was she also involved with Dutch? And what did that mean to Steve? To Marge? Even to Dutch?"

"Does it matter?"

"It might. All the promiscuity—" I couldn't stop the shiver of disgust "—could make for some hot, out-of-control jealousy, don't you think? A crime of passion."

Her hazel eyes met mine. "Control's important to you, isn't it? That's why you take lessons with Tyler, right?"

What my arrest hadn't done, those soft-spoken words did. For the second time in my life, I was powerless; once again someone else held my life in their hands.

I had no one to turn to, no one to hold me, no one to tell me everything would turn out right. I had no illusions.

Someone wanted me to take the fall for what they'd done. My most basic freedom was being stripped away, just as control of my body was once stolen from me.

They fingerprinted me. They swapped my skirt and top for a hideous orange thing. They even took away my Birkenstocks. I tried to pull away from what was happening, but everything felt like another blow.

Wilmont's small jail, located at the rear of the police station, was little more than a holding pen. After prisoners were processed, they were sent to the King County facility in Seattle if they couldn't post bail.

I had no money. I knew what was waiting for me.

Waiting was a hell all its own.

Once they'd labeled me a criminal, I huddled in the corner of the narrow bunk, the mattress barely more than a thin pad. I shivered, even though the day was hot. The cell was stuffy and the air too foul to breathe. The shivers started small, but as time crawled by, they grew. Soon I shook so hard that the bunk, bolted to the wall, creaked under me.

My heart pounded painfully. I had no control. I couldn't handle the misery, the confusion, the tragedy. Hysteria stole in and shut down my mind.

Some time later, I don't know how long, I heard my name. A familiar voice called me, but I was too far away. And I didn't want to go back. It hurt to go where that voice wanted me to go.

A warm hand touched my cheek, and I jerked away. I couldn't trust anyone. I had to hold them off . . . wrap my arms around me . . .

"Honey, please open your eyes."

Dad! He'd come. Just like the last time. He hadn't left me alone and devastated. He'd come.

Fear held me in its grip, but Dad's voice, the love in his words, proved stronger. I found the strength to open my eyes.

He sat at my side, on that crummy slab of wood the police called a bed. An age-spotted hand covered mine; the other touched my cheek again.

"Come on, honey. Let's go home."

"Home?" The voice didn't sound like mine, but the burning in my throat told me it was.

"Yes, Haley. We're going home."

"I'm in jail . . ."

"But we posted bail. You can come home now."

"Bail?" That meant money, right? "We don't have any . . ."

Dad's hands covered my fists where I held them tight around my knees. "It's okay, dear. The congregation insisted on paying your bail."

My eyes focused better now, but I still didn't understand. "How?"

"They took up a collection, then asked me to use the congregation emergency fund. They agreed this was the worst emergency our fellowship would ever face."

"They . . . did that . . . for me?"

"Yes, Haley. They did."

"But why?"

"Come on, honey. You have to stand up." His steady, gentle grip helped me rise. At first I felt dizzy. I almost fell. But Dad didn't let go.

"Why? Why'd they do that?"

He handed me my skirt. "Put this over your head. It's so long you can use it as a tent to change. I don't think you want to go back into the search room, do you?"

The memory of hands groping, touching me, brought panic back.

I hid under my skirt. The hideous orange thing came off. "Please, Dad. What made them pay for me?"

"Love, honey. That's what led them to do it. The love of Christ in their hearts."

"Aw, Dad—"

"No, Haley. You asked, and now you have to listen. I know how you feel about God, but it's my turn to speak. The love of Christ led them to do what they would have wanted, hoped, and prayed you would do for them had they been in your situation."

"The Golden Rule is just a cliché—"

"Absolutely not." I don't remember ever hearing my father as angry or as stern as he sounded right then. "That is the truth of the faith, Haley. It comes from God and is fed by his Word. That love leads to generosity that's otherwise impossible. The love of Jesus leads believers to see God in those they meet."

I tugged down the skirt. I tried to fight them, but the words

I'd learned in Sunday school came back to my lips. I hadn't gone after them, but they spilled from my lips of their own accord.

"Whatever you did for one of the least of these brothers of mine, you did for me."

13

Home was more than the place where they had to let you in no matter what. It really was a safe harbor. At least, it was for me. When I saw the manse again, I sobbed.

Dad stopped the car but didn't get out. He faced me, his expression thoughtful. When I didn't—couldn't—speak, he shook his head. "You've lost all faith, haven't you?"

I shrugged.

"How could you think I'd let you stay in jail? That no one cared enough to help you? You haven't fallen that low . . . have you?"

"Look, Dad, I know how you feel, but you also have to understand what I've been through. I don't see the goodness you say I'll find in people. It just hasn't been there for me. I can't even see the goodness you call God. The only good in my life has come from you, Mom, Marge, and Midas."

"That's a very bleak way to look at life."

"It's a realistic one from where I stand. Today should have shown you that."

"All I saw today was the police make a terrible mistake.

People make mistakes all the time. That's why we all have to acknowledge we're imperfect creatures."

When I said nothing, he went on. "Because of the police mistake, some good Christian folk showed their love by sharing what they have with us. You're free because of the love you deny."

I backhanded the tears off my chin. "I'll give you that much. But you'll have to let me tell you what I also saw in some of those people you say have so much love to give."

Dad reacted like I had to yesterday's gossip. But he didn't deny Penny's and Carla's accusations. "Marge had things in her past she wasn't proud of."

"She didn't warm a pew Sunday after Sunday either. She didn't go around looking for the church-lady-of-the-century award like they do. She wasn't a hypocrite."

"Marge wasn't a hypocrite, but she also didn't think she had any need for God's love and promises. She insisted this life was probably all there was. But she did qualify her statement. She always said probably."

"There's nothing more than a life that stinks and then you die, Dad. I haven't seen anything else."

"You haven't lived long enough."

"I've probably lived way too long. And if we don't get out of this car, my behind might just permanently bond itself to the vinyl upholstery." I stepped out. "I don't think I want to live out the rest of that life we're talking about right here."

He shook his head at my lame try but got out of the car too. "You might not want to hear it, Haley, but I'm going to say it every time I feel the Lord's leading." He locked the car door and went toward the porch. We both got there at the same time.

In the soft yellow glow from the lamp above the door, I noticed the lines around his eyes. They ran deeper than I remembered. This guilt I accepted. It was my fault Dad's day had been so hard.

But he wasn't done with me yet. "God loves you," he said, "and it's by his boundless grace that you're still here. There's a reason he spared you that other time. He won't let you down now either. You just have to reach out to him. He's waiting to take your hand again."

The familiar anger simmered to life, but this time, before I could take it and use it to my benefit, panic beat it down. My heart pounded hard and fast against my ribs. My throat closed down, all dry and scratchy and tight. My eyes burned, and my lungs couldn't draw air. My hands went cold, like blocks of ice.

I couldn't speak. I shook. Sweat beaded my forehead, and nausea made me heave. I lacked the strength to go up the porch steps.

Then the front door opened. In spite of the haze around me, Dad and someone else helped me up. Once inside, I blinked. My eyes began to clear. The man who'd come to our help was Tom. His face spoke volumes. He blamed himself for what had happened to me today.

"Oh, Tom . . ."

I couldn't go on. They led me to the couch, where Gussie waited, arms open wide.

"Come here, sweetheart. Let me hold you." Inside the comfort of her hug, I let the floodwaters flow. I don't know how long I cried, but Gussie never let me go. Dad patted my cheeks dry with an endless supply of tissues and poured the balm of tender words over my battered soul. Tom's silent presence helped me recover, especially when he brought me a cup of water and insisted I drink.

I couldn't deny their love. I also had to accept the mess I'd become. Not because I'd spent the day in jail and I stank, but because of my crashing emotions and the memories I couldn't stuff away.

"There's no easy way to say this," Dad started, "but you need help, Haley. More than I can give you, much more than what Tom and Gussie or any friend can offer. It's time for a trained professional, especially since you're still refusing God's healing touch."

"But—"

"Your father's right," Gussie said. "You're still fighting a four-year-old battle, and now you have a new one to fight. Don't go it alone any longer, sweetheart. There's help to be had. You just have to accept it."

Although I shook my head, I could hear Marge urging me to find a counselor, someone who specialized in helping victims of violence. "You can't just pretend it didn't happen," she'd said more times than I could remember. "Every time you push it away, you add another pound of trouble to your load. You have to face the bad, deal with it. Then you can go on."

Mom had said about the same thing, but she'd also said I should reach out to God first. She'd echoed Dad again and again.

I couldn't. I couldn't rake up the details of the attack. I

couldn't go through it again. But I also couldn't deny that I was in trouble. Dad, Tom, and Gussie knew it. So did I.

"I'll take care of it." I couldn't commit to anything. "But now I'd better get some rest. Whatever happens, I have to be ready. I won't be any good if I'm still this drained."

They watched me go upstairs. I concentrated on my steps. I made them steady, kept the shivers down to a shimmer or two, took deep, even breaths. Midas joined me, his solid bulk a comfort at my side.

Even though I didn't think I'd sleep, I was out almost before my head hit the pillow. I slept hard, and while dreams wafted in and out of my head, none stuck around long enough to form another nightmare. I just slept.

How come I felt so good the morning after a day that went so bad?

I couldn't figure it out, but when I opened my eyes, I felt better than I had since the day of the auction. A sliver of golden sunshine snuck in through the slit between the curtain panels on my window. I pulled them back and basked in the summer gold.

I had so much energy that, for lack of a better thing to do, I grabbed a dust cloth and a can of furniture spray and attacked dust bunnies with a vengeance. When every wood surface gleamed, I ran downstairs for a broom and went to town on the hardwood floor. As the final pièce de résistance, I rolled up my braided area rug, then unfurled it out the window. I shook it with all I had.

"Farewell, rabbits of the dust," I emoted. "There ain't no room for the two of us in this here town."

I laughed at my goofiness, and then couldn't stop from ripping out a song. "Oh what a beautiful morning, oh what a beautiful day . . ."

After I showered, I checked the clock. It was only ten o'clock. Wish I could be that productive all the time.

But then, I knew where that energy had come from, and I didn't want to do any more time in that deep, dark emotional pit.

"Okay," I told Midas. "Looks like I need a tune-up. Better get my gear and hustle to the *dojo*. And Tyler better not have some wimpy Tai Chi class going on. I want to kick and scream today."

I grabbed my bag, jumped in my Honda, and then zipped down the street. I turned right at the end of Puget Way, left on Pacific Drive, left again on Cedar Road, and finally squeaked a parking spot right across from Tyler's emporium of self-defense and sanity.

"Score!" The giddiness lingered. I hoped it lasted long enough to see me through the pounding of a bag, powerful kicks to man-height pads, lunges and parries, and the renewed sense of control.

I needed that today.

Tyler didn't disappoint. Johnny Weil was teaching a kick-boxing class. "Just what the doctor ordered," I told him as I hurried to the back of the group.

Johnny, who wore his hair bleached into a two-tone spiked-high Mohawk, gave me a weird look. "Whatever cleans your clock, Haley."

After we stretched and warmed up, I collared my nervous energy and fought like a woman possessed. No one got a jump on me. I could tell when I'd psyched them out enough to go in for the kill; I sniffed out their weaknesses. I took control of the class, and aside from Johnny, who, as teacher, didn't spar, I took everyone down.

When I stood in the center of the room, triumphant, breathless, and drenched in sweat, I spotted Tyler out of the corner of my eye. "Pretty good, don't ya think, *sensei*?"

"I think you'd better come into my office."

Great. He had more bad news for me. But today I was on a high. No one was going to bring me down. I walked into Asian World, as many of us called Tyler's lair, a cocky spring to my step.

Although Tyler took the corner of the couch, I was too pumped to sit still. I felt like a lioness, the undisputed queen of the jungle. I paced the long, narrow room from end to end.

When I felt ready for whatever he threw my way, I faced Tyler. "What's up?"

"The jig, Haley. The jig's up."

"Huh?"

"I've watched you play this game for years now, but Lila called me last night—"

"She shouldn't have arrested me—"

"That's not the issue, and you know it. I talked to your dad after I saw you go ballistic out there. If the others in class weren't as advanced as they are, you would've sent someone to the hospital today—"

"You're nuts! I was just better than everyone else today. And I didn't hurt anyone."

"By the grace of God, and not because you didn't try."

I went to object again, but the look he gave me brought me up short. I bit my bottom lip.

"You have a problem," he said, "and you have to do something about it. I'm not worried about you going to jail over Marge's murder. Lila'll find the killer, I promise you that."

He stood, came between me and the door. For a moment I feared his strength. Anger, disappointment, and power radiated from him in wave after wave after wave.

His voice, though soft, came laced with steel. "Ever since Marge brought you here four years ago, I've watched you. Yeah, what happened to you back then stinks, but you had a choice afterward. You could deal with it and go on and do something good with your life, or you could run from reality."

I glared. "I haven't run from anything, and I've done something good with my life. I've made it to brown belt and am on my way to black. No one's going to beat me up again. I even finished my interior design degree. I've opened my business, and Gussie's hired me. I'd say I've done some good stuff with my life."

"None of that's going to count in the long run. Especially not when the past still eats you up inside. You can't fight these accusations if you're still fighting demons from four years ago."

"Stop it! Just don't say anything more."

Ice chilled my veins. My hands shook. Red dots danced before my eyes, but a blurry kind of black swallowed them up. I fought the urge to vomit, and I wrapped my arms around myself.

"You don't know what it's like to be me." Each word hurt

more to get out than the last. "You don't know what it's like to be pinned, to be slammed again and again, for a hand to squeeze your throat, to know you're about to die because someone else wants something from you and they won't let you get in their way."

Helplessness burned deep in my soul. I gasped from the pain. When I could no longer hold the panic down, a cry tore free and I crumpled to the floor.

Did I black out? Did my brain take pity on me and shut down so I didn't have to relive the attack? I'll never know for sure, but I know I thrashed out with my arms and legs, fought the battle I'd lost four years ago. But this time, the man who victimized me was long gone. Tyler took a beating for that pig.

I only know that after a while I realized that Tyler had pinned me to the floor. His body covered mine, and his hands and feet kept me from flailing anymore. Even though he was in control, I had no strength to do anything about it. Besides, somewhere in the bowels of my mind, I realized Tyler would never hurt me. He was a rarity among men—he was a friend.

"Oh, Tyler . . ."

"Come on, girl. You know you can't go on like this." He rolled off and sat at my side.

I sobbed.

He stood, his feet shoulder-width apart. He held a hand out to me. "It's time you did something about this. Take my hand, Haley. Let me help you get your life back. You know you can trust me, you can trust the reverend, you can even trust Lila Tsu."

An automatic objection rushed to my lips, but I was trembling so much that I couldn't get it out. Tyler took advantage of my rare silence.

"No one, I mean no one, not me, not you, not any old person on this ugly old earth, can go it alone."

I tried to argue, but it came out like a moan.

He went on. "When you're sick, you go to a doctor. I know you do, because you've told me."

Tyler waited for me to respond, but I could only moan again. Even though I knew his compassion, he was dishing out his just as well-known tough love.

"You gotta get over this I-can-do-it-all-by-myself kick. You're sick inside, and not because of anything you did. But it *will* be on your shoulders if you do nothing about it. It's time to find a soul doctor and get some healing going on."

His words deflated any argument I might have mustered. I couldn't deny three meltdowns, one after the other.

"You're right." Fear made my teeth chatter so hard that I heard them hit each other. "I'm sick inside, and I don't know what to do about it anymore."

"First thing you gotta do, Haley, is take my hand. Get yourself up off that floor. Then look around you. Tell me what you see."

I didn't want to move. I wanted to curl up into a ball, grow a shell around me, one that could withstand a missile strike. That's it. I wanted to be a nuclear missile silo, impervious to attack, full of enough weapons that no enemy would strike first.

But you can't always get what you want. More than ever, I knew what the song really meant. I didn't think I'd ever hear it the same way again. And if Dutch used it as a stupid joke, I might . . . ah . . . I'd . . .

For the longest moment, I couldn't think of a thing that might teach Dutch some respect for those who suffered violence or the death of dreams. Then I had an idea, a brilliant one too. If he ever tried to joke about ruined hopes again, I'd take out my mace and zap him.

Just the thought gave me the strength to meet Tyler's gaze. His hand still waited for me. He'd never moved, never wavered in his determination to help me. Mom's and Dad's words rang in my mind. *"You have to reach out and take hold of that hand. It's waiting to help you get back on your feet."*

True, they'd meant God's hand, but they'd also talked of accepting the help others wanted to give me. Fighting fear with everything I had, I picked my arm up from the floor.

"Go ahead, Haley." Tyler's voice rang firm and encouraging. "Take my hand. Let me help you find your way back from the hell you've been in. There's hope, girl. And there are many of us who want to help you find it again."

Marge had said it.

Mom and Dad had too.

Even Detective Tsu had tried to make me see it.

Problem was, I knew nothing beyond the pain and the fear, beyond the stench of man's evil and the agony of God's betrayal.

Could I do it? Could I reach out and let others in?

It would take a lot from me, probably all I had.

It would take what I most lacked.

It would take faith . . . trust.

But I couldn't go on like this. I'd come to a turning point in my life. Whatever I did next would determine my future more than the capture of Marge's killer would. Which way should I turn?

I took Tyler's hand.

14

Faced with a new wardrobe dilemma, I chose another long cotton skirt and T-shirt to wear. Why didn't anybody tell a woman what she should wear to meet her new shrink?

I wasn't so sure about this whole spill-my-guts deal, but everyone else seemed to think I'd about achieved world peace by agreeing to meet the woman. Their reaction made me more willing to consider that maybe I really did need a psychologist's help.

I drove to the Sound and Sea Medical Building, my stomach in more knots than even my wild hair. Tyler had given me the shrink's name; she was a friend of his wife. Aside from that, he'd said nothing about the woman herself.

I knew she was a licensed counselor, that she shared Tyler's religious fervor, and that she wasn't Asian American like his wife, Sarah. At least, no Asian American I knew had a name like Teodora Rodriguez.

A blond guy about my age sat at the desk in the waiting room. I gave him my name, and he checked his computer screen. "You haven't been here before, have you?"

What gave him the first clue? That he'd never seen me

until today, or maybe it was my twisting fingers and darting glances. I was curious about the place, unhappy about being here, and looking for an escape route. I thought of Dad, Mom, Gussie, Tyler, Marge . . . there was no escape.

"Ah . . . no. You're right."

"You'll have to fill these out. Dr. Rodriguez will be with you as soon as you're done."

The door to his left opened. "It's all right, Ryan," the slender brunette said. "I've been expecting Haley. She can come right in, and we can take care of the paperwork while we talk."

What had Tyler told her that she'd break with office procedure just to get me in her inquisitive clutches? I wanted out even more than before.

But I'd recently learned one thing. I kept my mouth shut.

The look she gave me carried a load of humor. "Ty told me to expect the unexpected from you, but silence was the one thing he said I shouldn't expect."

"Tyler Colby thinks he knows everything."

"He does know everything often enough to be a little scary."

I laughed. "That's true."

She grinned, then stepped aside and waited for me to walk into her office. "Look, I know you didn't want to come, that your friends and family had to practically twist your arm to get you to make the call for the appointment."

"Face it," I countered on the defensive, "you're not exactly in the fun industry here. I doubt you're anybody's idea of a beautiful day in the neighborhood."

"True. But how many beautiful days have you had in your neighborhood lately?"

Surprisingly bright blue eyes sparkled at me, and although I didn't relax, at least I stopped looking to bolt. "Touché. So are you going to bring the sunshine back?"

"I'm going to help you see that the sunshine was there all along."

I snorted. "Maybe in your neighborhood."

"We only live a few blocks apart."

"Not hardly. No woman wants my address. Trust me."

"I was told I could. Have you heard you can trust me too?"

"How can I? You've no idea where I'm coming from."

Dr. Rodriguez sat in a comfortable armchair and indicated the matching one for me. Phew! No couch. I couldn't have laid down for a nanosecond.

With a sad smile, she opened a manila folder and took out a sheet of paper. It looked sickly familiar. My stomach churned.

She set copies of the police report and my attacker's sentencing records on the Queen Anne cherry coffee table between us. "I hope you forgive me, but I took the liberty to check public records. Tyler said you were the victim of a violent crime little more than four years ago. I found the paper trail."

She stared until I had no choice but to meet her gaze. "I know exactly where you're coming from. I was also raped, when I was twenty years old."

That evening, Dad and I went to the Stoker home for dinner. After the turbulent morning, it was about the only place I could imagine going. I had too much on my mind.

Dr. Rodriguez—Tedd, as she'd asked me to call her—had pulled no punches. After she'd dropped her bombshell, she'd told me her tale. At the end, I'd known she understood most of what I'd gone through. The difference was she'd been raped by a stranger, and in a confrontation with the police, he'd been shot and killed.

Paul Campbell had been my boyfriend. Date rape is no less rape just because you know the guy that forces himself on you, steals your right to decide, steals something even more precious than that. Paul stole my innocence, my sense of trust, my faith, and any hope I'd had for the future.

He got probation and forty hours of community service.

Even though I'd heard he'd left Washington, at any given time he could show up again. That didn't make a woman feel any too secure. Not this woman.

But Tedd understood my rage. She understood my need for control. She knew why I fell apart under ridiculous accusations and, ultimately, when my freedom was ripped from me as the cell walls and bars closed in on me.

She let me scream. She gave me tissues. She even had Ryan run across the street to get me a Starbucks venti caramel macchiato. From what she said, she'd cleared her morning of other sessions to give me as much time as I needed.

I don't know how I made it home afterward. I'd felt like a wrung-out dishrag when we were done. On the excuse that I had to finish my presentation for the Stokers' redesign, I took refuge in my room and crawled into bed. The adrenaline drain left me so weak that I slept like a log.

Now, portfolio in hand, I sat on the passenger side of Dad's Taurus as we drove the three blocks between our home and the Stokers'.

The veal marsala was excellent. So was the boysenberry

pie, made from berries that Gussie had canned herself. Now, there was a woman who didn't let even a debilitating disease keep her from doing what she wanted. As we walked into the living room, where I'd do my bada-bing thing, I realized that I'd have to become more like Gussie if I wanted to move forward with my life.

"I hope you and Tom like what I've put together for you." The easel held my design-board upright, and I liked how it had turned out. I started my pitch. "I'd like to move the furniture away from the walls, Gussie. That'll give you more room to maneuver on those days when you're forced to use the wheelchair all the time. . . ."

They loved the soft and comfy chenille for the sofa, and the luxurious gleam of the dupioni silk inspired sighs of pleasure. The sassy persimmon stripe and the luscious taupe and cream and gold tapestry also got me a bunch of oohs and aahs. The see-through Thai silk, however, was my coup de grâce.

"I've never seen anything like it," Gussie said, gaze glued to the beautiful fabric. "I can't wait to see it on the windows."

"Here," I said. "Let me put it up against this one here. It'll at least give you an idea of how the sunset's going to look once the draperies are in place."

The current curtains were heavy, pinch-pleated antique satin. A full lining made sure no light came through them unless they were pulled all the way back. Since the window faced the street, Gussie and Tom kept them closed for the sake of privacy.

I tugged on the cord, and the setting sun's russet glow poured in. The knick-knacks on the table in front of the

window took me a minute to move out of my way. I was
tall, but I still needed help to reach the hardware. I took off
my Birkenstocks, turned to wink at the Stokers and Dad,
climbed the table, and then held the edge of the silk up to the
rod. The yard-length of fabric I'd wheedled from Adrienne
for demo purposes was just enough to give the illusion of
a curtain.

At Gussie's sigh of delight, I smiled. "To be honest, it looks
even better than I thought it would. I chose the color scheme
because these windows face the west. I wanted to make the
most of the gorgeous sunsets you'll be able to enjoy once I'm
done with the installation."

"Haley," Dad said. "I knew you had a multitude of abili-
ties and more talent than you knew what to do with, but I
have to give you credit. This is spectacular. You've outdone
yourself."

Pleasure rippled through me—a foreign feeling these last
few days. "Thanks, Dad." I turned to my potential clients.
"So . . . do I get the job?"

Tom laughed. "You had the job and our trust from the start,
but now that we've seen what you have in mind, there's not
a soul out there who stands a chance. How soon can you
start?"

Oh yeah, oh yeah. I had a job. "Since I'm otherwise unemployed—" I rolled my eyes "—I can start tomorrow. I'll place
the order for the fabrics and call the furniture showroom for
the new case goods."

I went to fold the Thai silk, but Gussie stopped me. "Could
I keep that sample? At least until the room's done. I want to
dream on it, honey."

How could I deny her? "Of course. Tell you what. I'll drape the others around the room. You know, in the areas where I plan to use the specific pieces. That way you can live with the new concept for a while and make sure it's right for you."

"Oh, that's a better idea," Gussie exclaimed. "Here. See if there's some way to keep the curtain fabric folded over the rod. You know, something like what you just did."

Back at the window, I again kicked off my Birkenstocks and hopped on the table. A few pins later, I asked, "How's this?"

"Perfect," Tom replied. "Now be careful on your way down. We don't want anything to happen to our wonderful designer."

"Oh, goodness, Tom," Gussie chided. "Don't even think that. We'll just have to take care of our Haley. And not because she's our designer or because of what she's going to do here. She's just a wonderful girl, an absolute darling."

Embarrassed, I crept back down, and began to rearrange Gussie's tchotchkes. Millefiori paperweights fascinated me. Even though I knew glassblowers inserted rods of colored glass into balls of the melted clear glass, I still found the little colored flowers inside solid glass almost miraculous.

The Limoges porcelain pitcher and its fresh roses came next. They smelled wonderful. Then I picked up a figurine. I'd noticed its unusual weight when I'd moved it to a side before, but now I took time to check it out.

It looked like it came from the 1920s, a bronze of a woman, as stylized as art-deco pieces tend to be. It was more than exquisite. It was a true work of art, a treasure.

And familiar.

If memory served me right, the piece was an Erté, created by the famous French sculptor. Many of his pieces depicted graceful women in poses that spoke of his time. And the reason I recognized it so easily was because it had been listed in the catalog for the Gerrity auction.

I put the pricey bauble back on the table. I hadn't realized that the Stokers had purchased the piece. I hadn't thought they could afford something that sold for thousands of dollars and whose peers graced museums all over the world.

True, it was tarnished on one side, maybe dirty, actually, but patina was important in order to date a piece and determine its authenticity. This one looked as real as real could get.

But something tickled the back of my memory. No matter how hard I tried, I couldn't remember Marge actually offering the piece at the sale. I went to ask Gussie about the Erté, but embarrassment held me back.

What if it wasn't the one from the sale? What if they'd had the statuette for years? What kind of designer would miss such a distinctive piece in someone's décor? Especially in a house she'd visited umpteen jillion times. I didn't want to look like some kind of no-clue amateur, so to be on the safe side, I decided to stop by the warehouse the next day and check out the catalog.

Not long after my rousing beginner's success, Dad and I loaded my board and portfolio into the car and drove home.

The only words spoken were Dad's quiet, "I'm so proud

of you, Haley. You took enormous steps toward your future today. I'll keep praying for your progress, honey."

I hoped no new attack derailed that progress I so needed to make.

I rubbed my eyes. Amazing what squinting at a computer screen could do to you. And I'd been at it for hours. No matter how hard I looked, I couldn't make the facts add up. Just as I'd thought, the Erté was listed in the sale catalog. But as I'd also suspected, there was no record of it going up for sale, and certainly none of a buyer.

If Marge was known for anything, it was for her attention to detail. She wouldn't have let a discrepancy that big stand, not even for a short intermission.

"Ozzie?" I called reluctantly. I didn't know what to think of him now that I'd read that awful memo. "Can I ask you something?"

"Of course. How can I be of service, Miss Farrell?"

If things ever worked out that I'd own this place, we'd have to shake him up some. That Miss Farrell thing got old real quick.

"I remembered a piece from the catalog, a beautiful sculpture, and I wondered who'd bought it."

He rubbed his chin and then smiled. "Oh, you mean the Erté. She is stunning, isn't she?"

"Lovely." But not what I wanted. "Do you know who bought it?"

His forehead furrowed again—no smile though. "Come to think of it, miss, I cannot recollect . . . I don't even know if it sold."

I knew enough to keep my big mouth shut.

He shook his head as though to clear it of cobwebs. Poor man. There were no cobwebs. If what I'd already checked out turned out to be true, then the figurine had never gone up for bid.

"If you'll give me but a moment, I'd like to verify something in the database."

As he walked away, muttering under his breath, a weird sensation started in the pit of my stomach. If the Erté hadn't sold, then how did it wind up in the Stokers' living room? And why?

What did it mean? Did it mean anything?

Had I finally gone off the deep end?

After about fifteen minutes of similar ring-around-the-rosy thoughts, Ozzie returned, the worried look back in place, the same one he'd worn when he couldn't find Marge at the auction.

Things were getting kinda squirrelly again. "What's wrong?" I asked when I couldn't stand the wait a second longer.

"It's the strangest thing, Miss Farrell—"

"For Pete's sake, Ozzie! Stop with the Miss Farrells already. You've known me since I was a snot-nosed little kid. You'd think you could make yourself call me Haley by now."

He took a step back. "I do apologize, Miss—er . . . ah . . . Haley. It was never my intent to offend."

Did I blow that or what? "Ozzie, you didn't offend me, but you make me feel as if I have parsley stuck between my teeth, stepped on dog poop, and tracked it into Buckingham Palace while I did some kind of whirling dervish dance."

His eyes widened even more. "I . . . I . . ."

"Look. All I'm saying is that you don't have to be so formal around me. Just call me Haley, and we'll get along fine, as fine as we always have."

"Very well, M—er . . . Haley."

"Good! See? The ground didn't even open up under you or anything." Now, here was a guy without a sense of humor. But he did have info I needed. "You were saying about the sculpture . . . ?"

"Oh! Yes. It's the oddest thing. There's no record of it selling. Now, it's a rare occurrence when an item, especially one so desirable, doesn't sell, but it does happen from time to time." He shook his head again. "What's truly odd is that we have no record of Marge putting it up for bid during the auction. It was scheduled as one of the last pieces before the intermission."

"What do you think happened?"

"I can't begin to imagine. Perhaps . . ."

When he'd mulled his thoughts long enough, I stuck in an impatient, "Yes . . . ?"

"The only thing I can think of is that the runners—you know, the teens who help bring the smalls up front during the sale—couldn't find it. They might have told Werner, our catalog man, and he could have told Marge we'd have to leave it until the afternoon. The piece created enough interest to warrant a special sale."

"Funny no one's mentioned it. I mean, since it was such a favorite and all."

He nodded, the glum look back on his plain features. "I know precisely what you mean. I can't imagine why I didn't remember."

"Give me a break, Ozzie. Give yourself a break." At his puzzled look, I went on. "You only went through your employer's murder, an investigation, and then you got called out to inventory an estate for possible sale. When have you had time to remember a tchotchke that didn't sell?"

"Miss Farrell—*Haley!* An Erté is much more than a . . . a mere knickknack. It's an absolute treasure. It should never have slipped my mind."

"Give it a rest. If I sweated every last thing I forgot, then there wouldn't be enough soap by half to go around the world. Pretty stinky, don't you think?"

Ouch! Lame.

But he smiled. True, it looked more like the kind one gives a nutcase, the "Let's humor the poor dear" kind. But hey. I did get him to smile. I added, "Time to go. I have a bunch of stuff to buy for the redesign I'm doing."

On my way out, Ozzie called and asked me the single, solitary question I'd hoped he wouldn't ask.

"Since the sculpture did not sell," he said, "and since we have no record of it being offered, and especially since I know it isn't on the premises, then where do you think it's gone?"

Since I couldn't answer, refused to do so, I shrugged and fled, coward that I am. That uneasy feeling prowled around my middle again. I didn't want to deal with it right then.

Yeah, right. I didn't want to deal with it, period. End of story.

So I made a beeline for the cop shop. Let the unflappable—love that word; I'd never used it before, but now I thought of Detective Tsu as the unflappable karate chop cop—Detective Tsu figure it all out.

Still, I scored another victory. Chalk two in one day for the prime suspect in a murder case. I ran into the police department, dashed past the receptionist/dispatcher, who watched, jaw gaping, eyes horrified. Then I zipped past a group of Smurf cops and flung open the door with the brass plaque that read, in large block letters, "Captain Lila Tsu," and in small letters, "Homicide."

She'd been at her desk, wire-rimmed glasses on the bridge of her nose. She gasped and stood in a hurry, her actions for once awkward and graceless. The chair rolled back and hit the file cabinet to the right rear of the desk before it toppled over. It might have clipped her leg on its way down.

But just that fast, the unflappability was back in place. "What are you doing here?"

"A clue!"

I startled her again, but she did a good job disguising it. "Excuse me?"

"I have a clue . . . a lead . . . whatever you want to call it. And this is one you didn't know before."

The elegant eyebrow rose. "I wouldn't be so sure, Haley. I'm very thorough."

"I bet you are, but this has nothing to do with thoroughness. It has to do with antiques and the sale and what did and didn't sell."

"Care to run that by me again?"

"I'm not going to waste time like that." I took a deep breath to tamp down my excitement. Maybe this was the pass I needed to get out of jail free, like in Monopoly. "I found something where it shouldn't be, a piece that should've sold but didn't. And it's in the last place you'd think it'd wind up."

"I thought you weren't going to waste time." Detective Tsu smiled, taking some of the sting out of her words. "Why don't you tell me what the item is, where it is, and why it shouldn't be there. I especially want to know how you discovered it and why you think it's in the wrong place."

Faster than a toddler after a crystal vase, I told her about my presentation. She grinned when I mentioned the table I climbed. Bet she didn't go around climbing on suspects' side tables, no matter what. Then I told her about the Erté, how valuable it was, how it had been listed but hadn't sold.

"It is puzzling," she said when I ran out of steam, "but I don't see where it has anything to do with the case. Not unless you know more than you're telling."

That popped-balloon feeling hit again. "I only know what I told you, but don't you think it's significant that a piece that never went up for bid at the auction turned up in the Stokers' living room?"

"Significant how?"

"What if someone meant to steal the piece, Marge found them, they bashed in her head, and then, when I started screaming, they ditched it in the Stokers' things. You know, so that they wouldn't be caught with incriminating evidence."

"It's plausible," Ms. Tsu said, throwing a wet blanket on my excitement, "but highly unlikely."

That made me mad. "Why? Because it would clear me?"

"Not necessarily, Haley. Think about it. You *say* you just found the statue at the Stokers' house. That *you*'d never noticed it there before. And now *you* also want me to consider it the key to the murder, the one *you're* accused of committing. How does that sound to you now?"

Frustration brought bitter tears to my eyes. "It sounds as though you're determined to lock me up for life. Even though new evidence has now turned up."

"Look, I'm not 'determined,' as you say. I'm just telling you what a judge and a jury are going to think." She took a deep breath. "They're also likely to turn against you for this."

"What do you mean?"

"How would you react if someone who looked guilty as sin tried to shift the blame onto a disabled woman and the husband who cares for her?"

"But that's not what I'm doing . . ."

Nothing I said would change her mind. I saw it in her eyes.

I squared my shoulders. "Think what you want, but I know something strange is going on here. And I'm going to figure it out. Then, Karate Chop Cop, when you're washing the egg off your face, don't say I kept evidence from you. Remember, I tried to feed it to you, but you spat it back out."

I retraced my earlier steps, excusing myself to all I'd

shocked. Polite as my departure was, it wouldn't gain me a thing, not a minute less of jail time, that's for sure. The only thing that would save me was a miracle. And I'd have to work that myself.

I had no other choice.

15

Running ideas someone's already termed wild past your very serious-minded, ultraconservative, logical, absolutely nonsuspicious father is not a smart thing. I, of course, did just that as soon as I got home. I wanted Dad to agree with me, to say that something strange was going on, that maybe I'd found the key to turning suspicion elsewhere.

But he didn't.

He reacted as Detective Tsu had.

"I know you're worried about going back to jail," he said. "But really, dear. This is terrible. How can you accuse the Stokers of murder? One would think you of all people wouldn't throw around accusations like that."

"Why does everyone think I'm accusing *them*?" I blew hair out of my eyes. The rebellious, fluffy stuff wafted back down to where it had started out.

I went on, certain I was on the right track. "All I said is that someone stole the statue, probably killed Marge when she caught him. Then, when I found the body, he stashed the thing where he knew no one would think to look for it."

"That's crazy."

"No, really. Would you think Gussie or Tom might stuff a chunk of brass worth thousands inside the bag on the back of the wheelchair?"

"You don't know that's what happened. No one but you would come up with that thought."

"Bingo! That's my point. No one else would think to look there for evidence either." I scored that point. "But I bet the killer did. He also probably thought he could get it back when the cops were done with him. I doubt he thought Detective Karate Chop—"

"Who?"

"You know. The perfect woman who decided she's going to get me no matter what." At his puzzled look, I added, "Lila Tsu, Dad. The homicide detective in charge of Marge's murder investigation."

"You mean that nice young woman who takes lessons with you at Tyler's gym?"

I didn't know which error to address first, calling Detective Tsu nice or calling Tyler's *dojo* a gym, so I corrected neither. "Yeah, sure. That one. Anyway, you want to bet the killer never thought the cops would send Tom and Gussie home right away?"

"You know I don't bet, Haley, but that could be true. Not that I think the sculpture matters in the long run."

"Then how did it get to Gussie's living room? Who do you think got it there? Or do you think the Stokers mysteriously bought it from Marge, and she never bothered to record the sale, much less tell Ozzie about it?"

"Don't you think the Stokers would have wondered how the figurine got in their bag? Into their living room?" He shook his head and gave me an indulgent smile. "I'm sure there's a logical explanation, just as I'm sure there's a God in heaven who'll reveal the truth in his own good time."

"Let me tell you, Dad. I hope you're right, and I sure hope he hurries. If he doesn't, I'm going to stink in that cell worse than Lazarus did after lying around dead until Jesus got there to raise him up . . . from the . . . dead . . ."

Where did that come from? Yet another time in recent days that Scriptural scraps floated up from my past. It shocked me enough that I shrugged, kissed Dad on the head, and ran upstairs.

Maybe something strange *was* happening.

But was it happening to me?

By the time my next session with Tedd rolled around, I'd begun to question my own sanity. Why not? Everyone else did.

But the savvy Latina shrink asked the one question no one else had. "Do *you* think you're losing your mind? Do you think you're imagining bogeymen where there aren't any?"

I stared at her, another elegant woman, but this one originally so. Whereas Detective Tsu did nothing to enhance her ethnic beauty, Tedd left no doubt in anyone's mind how she felt about her heritage. Rich, glossy black waves tumbled past her shoulders, held back by a pair of hand-hammered silver combs, one at each side of her center part. Ruby lipstick enhanced her full lips, and a white blouse, embroidered in the same fiery shade, hinted at athletic curves. More Taxco silver graced her earlobes, wrists, fingers, and throat. Everything she wore showed pride in the artistry of fellow Mexicans.

But she'd asked a question, and no matter how I tried to avoid it, she'd made a good point. "No, I'm not losing my mind. At least, I don't think I am when someone who refuses to see what's so clear to me doesn't tell me I am."

"And when they do . . . ?"

"Then I question my motives. Am I that desperate to avoid jail that I would blame an even more innocent person? Have I really fallen that low?"

Tedd waited in silence. She'd made it clear, in words and actions, that she wasn't going to give me any answers. She felt that any she offered wouldn't be mine and wouldn't benefit me.

I looked at my hands, hands that had moved the Erté, hands that had clutched the rock that crushed Marge's skull, hands that had once tried to fight off a man bent on domination and self-gratification. How could anyone use their hands to hurt or kill another?

"There is a bogeyman," I said. "But he's not in my imagination. He killed Marge, and he's waiting for me to pay for his crime."

"And the sculpture?"

"Ozzie Krieger, Marge's assistant, agrees that something happened to that statue. And he doesn't know I found it, that it turned up at the Stoker home."

"Would he play mind games with you? Could he be guilty?"

"Could be. I just know what I know."

Tedd's ability to get me to cut to the chase impressed me. I'd come to our session questioning what I'd seen. She'd let me talk things out, and I no longer questioned myself. I doubted anyone could budge me now.

"How do you think the rape has affected how you see this crime?"

I inhaled sharply. "I haven't given it thought."

"Take your time and think about it now."

It didn't take long to find an answer. "I think the rape colors everything I see, think, or do. I don't know that it can ever be different."

"What if I told you that's not a bad thing?"

"I'd think we need to swap chairs."

She chuckled. "Think about it, Haley. You have a different way of looking at this murder. You even have a different perspective than a jaded detective. In this case, that perspective might prove to be a benefit."

"I wouldn't go that far."

"I would, and that's because I've been in your shoes. Don't you think my experience helps me understand others? To walk that mile in their shoes?"

"I guess, but I don't see where that follows in my case."

"I'd suggest that the suspicion everyone's directed at you is a way to ward off fear."

She blocked my objection with a shake of her head. "Give me a chance to explain myself. Everyone, even a cop, is capable of fear. Murder is the ultimate violence, the ultimate fear everyone has to conquer. They need a quick answer to the question at the top of their thoughts, and they need it right away. Who killed Marge becomes greater than the need to know. For most, it boils down to knowing who might kill again. And will it be me or someone I love he kills next?"

"I can sort of buy that, but I don't see where I'm all that

different. Except that I'm more afraid I'll wind up in jail with no way to help myself."

"Exactly. You've been to the edge of death and, by the grace of God, came back from it. It's lack of freedom and control that rocks you."

I nodded. She understood.

"Can't you see that while others are ready to jump to the quickest solution, you can distance yourself and see more? You can question the easy answers. To see everyone who's involved in a different light."

"That's some way to make lemonade out of the sourest lemons."

"That's what life is all about, Haley." Tedd's grin was infectious.

I smiled back in spite of myself.

"Think about it," she added. "I'm sure that, as a preacher's kid, you're familiar with Scripture. The one that comes to mind right now is the one that speaks about keeping our minds on what is worthy, beautiful, etc. Those of us who can do that after something as repulsive as rape are the ones who survive."

Of course I knew Philippians 4:8—one of Dad's favorites. "Let me ask you something, and I really want an answer."

"I'll see what I can do," Tedd replied, serious now.

"Why do you guys always bring it back to the God stuff? I don't get it. How can you still have faith when he left you out to hang? He didn't stop that monster from doing what he wanted."

"God could have stopped the rapes, yours and mine. But would I have become the woman I am today without it? I doubt it. Once upon a time, the only thing in my mind was to sing my way to the top of the charts. And I wasn't singing God's praises either. Now I can serve him and his children in need. You tell me what's better."

"You're telling me I should be glad Paul raped me because it's going to make me a better person?"

"Not at all. I'm suggesting that you quit fighting so hard. Don't fight God, and don't fight the reality of what happened. Let God redeem what that locust stole from you. Use it to benefit the kingdom. You'll never be at peace until you do."

I felt need. I wanted that peace more than I'd ever wanted anything in my life. I wanted it even more than I'd wanted to escape Paul's hands, his attack, his violation.

"You want me to accept God's betrayal—"

"I'm telling you to stop seeing that man's criminal decision as God's action in your life. Sin is sin, Haley. God didn't make Paul rape you. He chose to do that by himself. Until you put the blame where it belongs, you'll never reach a place where God can heal you."

Tears filled my eyes. "So what's the prescription, Doc?"

"I don't have the answer. Only God does, and you're going to have to work out your salvation from the hell you're in through the power of his love." She reached out and hugged a worn leather Bible. "God calls us to recognize the evil around us, forgive those who hurt us, and move on to fight the good fight for him. You have to face your past to resolve your feelings about it. Then you'll be able to deal with the present, and someday face your future."

"Did you go to the same seminary where Dad went?" My voice was shaky, but at least I spoke. Her words had hit me with a rush of uncertainty, not about what she said, but about the thoughts I'd clung to for the last four years.

Tedd gave me another brilliant smile. "I went to shrink school. But I do go to church, read my Bible, and check in with God about everything. I bet your dad does the same."

"I wish . . ." My watch said I didn't have to finish my thought. The session was over. "Look at the time! Your next client must be ready to skin me alive, I've made you so late."

In my hurry to leave the aching wish behind, I snagged my backpack purse and practically ran to the door.

"Haley."

I screeched to a stop.

"Don't leave until you finish your wish."

How had I known she was going to do that? I sighed but didn't face her. "I wish I had your faith."

I closed the door and left before Tedd could see my tears.

Two days later I'd finished making the Stokers' living-room window treatments. I packed my super-duper steamer into the car, then spread the silks across the backseat. I did what I could to minimize creases, but the steamer would make the fabric look wonderful when I hung it up.

I couldn't wait to put the curtains in place. The case goods had been delivered, and I'd had the rest of the furniture moved to the new floor plan. Already the room looked much better. Today I was going to add that touch of elegance Gussie wanted.

I'd thought the sessions with Tedd would make me less able to cope, that the memories would keep me from normal function, but the opposite turned out to be the case. It seemed that the more garbage I dumped in her office, the stronger I grew. Go figure.

The drive was short and pleasant, but the arrival left a lot to be desired.

I gave the steering wheel a couple of light whacks with my forehead. When I looked up again, the mirage was no mirage.

Dutch stood on the sidewalk outside Gussie's home, grim faced, arms crossed. Was he trouble or what?

Then I remembered the threat I'd made. No way was he going to ruin my mood. I reached into my backpack purse and grabbed my trusty can of mace . . . or maybe it was the pepper spray. It didn't matter. Either would do the job.

I got out of the car. "Hey there, sunshine. Does a body good to see your smiling mug."

"Stuff the sarcasm. I have a couple of questions for you."

"Uh-uh. You don't get to ask any. That's the cops' job."

"I can ask anything I want, and if you're smart, you'll answer. Even though I know you're guilty as sin, we both want the same outcome."

"First of all, I'm not guilty as sin. And second, there's no way you know what I want, so you're off base on that one too."

"You want Noreen to buy the Gerrity, don't you?"

It had been so long since I'd thought of the mansion as a

potential job, that I shrugged. "I'd much rather find Marge's killer, if you want to know the truth."

"You don't want the job?"

"There are bigger things in life."

"That *is* my life."

"Then, buddy boy, you better get a life." I started up the walk, ready to end the inane exchange.

"What's this about you planting a so-called clue in these people's home?" he asked.

"Where'd you hear that? Who'd you harass into saying that?"

Could he make a woman mad or what? "Either you're stupid or you're deaf, dumb, and blind. And the dumb part has more than one meaning. I didn't plant anything."

"I know what I heard."

"Then you need to Q-Tip your ears more often. You heard wrong, wrong, wrong."

"So tell me what's right, right, right."

I took comfort in my can of mace. "The last time I was here, I found a sculpture I recognized from the auction catalog. I went to the warehouse, checked the catalog and computer, and verified that the piece never went up for sale. Yes, it is the same sculpture. There's only one in the world."

"So how did it get from there to here?"

"That's what I want to find out."

"More dumpster diving?"

"Wanna check out how well mace works?"

One long step back later, he said, "You're nuts, you know? Wacko, loony tunes, and stark raving mad."

"Yeah, I'm mad. I'm mad because you and a bunch of others can't see what's dangling off the tips of your noses. A sculpture wandered off the grounds of the Gerrity estate, and because it's worth so much, I'd be willing to bet someone stole the thing. They're probably just waiting for the right moment to pop in and get it back."

"Good try."

"It is good. Ever hear of a botched robbery? People can wind up dead during those."

That brought him up short. For a moment, he looked like he was about to lob another zinger my way. Then, to my surprise, he nodded slowly. "It's nuts, but I see where you might be right."

"All righty, then. Give the man a cigar! He sees the light."

"Forget the cigar. Just give me a contract and a chance to vindicate myself. And don't interfere with my efforts to get my career back on its feet."

"I won't interfere. So long as you don't try to convince me I'm guilty of a murder I didn't commit."

His nod was sweet victory. And I hadn't had to use the mace.

Yet.

He took a step closer. "So what's the verdict on the statue?"

"Right now it's a matter of wait and see. I couldn't talk Karate Chop Cop into following up on the lead."

"Karate . . . Chop . . ." He sputtered with laughter. "I gather Ms. Tsu is into martial arts."

"She studies at the same *dojo* where I do."

"You're into that stuff too?"

My smile was wide and mischievous. "Better watch it,

buddy boy. You tick me off again, and it's mace or kickboxing for you."

"And you're into floor plans, froufrou, and paint too?"

"They call it multifaceted, don't ya know?"

He chuckled again. "So you'll let me know if you learn
anything else about the sculpture?"

"I have nothing to lose by telling you. Unless *you* killed
Marge."

"Don't start that again."

I raised my arms. "Truce."

He went for my mace.

I moved faster.

A moment later, Dutch lay flat on his back in the Stokers'
front yard. I could almost see little yellow canaries circling
his head.

Uh-oh. I'd gone too far. Would he press charges?

But instead of crying foul, Dutch sat up and laughed.
"That'll teach me to mess with Karate Chop Suspect."

"Watch it, buster." I held out a hand.

A hungry rattler would've been a worthier recipient of his
look. He hauled himself up. "We'd be farther ahead if instead
of sniping at each other, we decided to cooperate."

I looked him over. "Sounds good to me."

He held out a hand. Instead of shaking, I turned it palm up
and gave him the mace. "You have yourself a deal."

"I'll wait for your call."

"You call me if you hear anything new."

We said good-bye, and as he went to his truck, he detoured
past the driver's side of mine. "Take note, Haley." He tossed
the mace inside. "In the spirit of cooperation."

I chuckled, ran up the steps, and rang the doorbell. The whir of the wheelchair's motor announced Gussie.

We wasted no time hanging the curtains. They looked even better than I'd hoped. Gussie loved them.

"You're brilliant," she said about a dozen times. "And I have no doubt about your innocence. You did not kill Marge Norwalk."

We hadn't mentioned the murder, but her vote of confidence warmed my heart. "Thanks, Gussie. Your opinion means a lot."

"I've said it before, and I'll tell you again. You're a wonderful young woman, Haley. You hold a special place in my heart. It's almost as if God's given me you at this time almost to make up for the son I lost."

"Gussie . . . I'm so sorry. I didn't know you'd had a child."

Her bottom lip quivered. "I went into labor prematurely. It was a difficult pregnancy, and by the time he was born, he was dead."

Her grief brought tears to my eyes. "I didn't know . . ."

"We don't talk about it much. It's still hard."

"I can imagine." Acting on impulse, I wrapped my arms around her. Gussie clung to me, her sobs silent, her pain only too real.

When her tears were spent, I gave her the box of tissues she kept by the overstuffed armchair near the fireplace. "It's your turn today. I'm glad I was here just as you were there for me."

"Thank you, honey. You don't know how much it means to me."

When I left a short while later, I thought about Gussie's

loss. What could it be like for your child to die? Did that hurt as much as what Paul did to me? I saw where it might.

And that's when I understood some of what Tedd had tried to make me see. Even though I hadn't experienced the death of a child, my loss helped me understand Gussie's grief.

For the first time, the memory of the rape didn't bring me down. Maybe that redeeming thing Tedd had talked about had begun.

16

When I got home, I was so deep in thought that I paid no attention to what I was doing. I stabbed myself with my sewing scissors. Blood poured from the gash, and I realized how deep and long the cut was.

It hurt.

I needed medical attention, but I hated hospitals with a passion. I'd spent a miserable week in one after the rape, and the memories were bleak and haunting.

No matter how I felt, I had to get to a doctor soon. And no way could I drive like this. Dad's car wasn't in the driveway. He wasn't at the church either.

I looked up and down the street. Pavarotti's distinctive tenor soared from Bella's open windows. On my way over, I wondered where her monster cat was.

She answered the doorbell on the second bong. "Haley! What'd you do to yourself?"

"My scissors got me. I need a favor. Could you drive me—"

"Awwwright! Always wanted to drive an ambulance. Get in my car, and I'll get you there in a flash."

She wanted the hospital, but it was my hand, after all. I won that battle, but she won the other one—as we burned rubber out of her driveway, she clamped a magnetic cherry light to the top of her 1965 vintage pink Caddy.

I clung to the door handle for dear life. When we hit a straight stretch, I called old Doc Cowan, the man who had delivered me. "Can you sew me up in the office?"

"How soon can you get here?"

"I'm a block away."

"I'll be waiting."

Bella pouted about the doctor's office. I knew she cared about my hand, but I knew her too well. She wanted the drama of the emergency room, the nurses and aides running to my rescue, the rush of flying down the hall to a curtain-draped cubicle. Never mind that I wasn't anywhere near death.

Doc Cowan shook his head when he saw my hand. "What have you been up to, Haley girl?"

I told him about my day. But only the good parts. It helped pass the time until the local anesthetic took hold. Then as he embroidered my hand, I mentioned Gussie's miscarriage.

"That was sad," he said. "She was distraught. What's worse is that she tore inside and nearly bled to death. Then she didn't heal right. That's why she never had another child. It's common knowledge. Has been since it happened."

Another loss for Gussie, this one of a dream.

Doc shook his head. "I've wondered a time or two what kind of results we might have had if today's technology had been available."

"Do you think you could have saved the baby?"

"Maybe not the infant, but we might have preserved her fertility. It affected her entire life, changed her completely. She reacted with strange, unacceptable behavior for a while. It nearly ruined her marriage too."

"But Tom's devoted to her!"

"True. But a man can only take so much trouble at one time. He blamed himself for the miscarriage. Then too, Gussie's antics reached the point where she had to come to her senses or one of them was going to land in jail."

"Gussie took up a life of crime?"

"Ah . . . listen to me. I'm running off at the mouth like some old biddy who's got nothing better to do than gossip her time away."

"No, really, Doc. Did Gussie break the law?"

"Why do you ask?"

"Because it might explain how she understands my fears." And more. "You know the police think I killed Marge, don't you?"

"What a load of manure! I couldn't believe it when I read the paper." Doc snipped the suture thread, tossed the needle into a hazardous waste can, then stripped his gloves and did the same. "Don't cops have more sense than that?"

"That's what I've said from the start." But the last few days and two wily brunettes had taught me much. "Don't change the subject, Doc. Did Gussie get in trouble with the law?"

"It was minor stuff, but yes. She had a brush with the law at the time—you can go check old police records."

"Poor Gussie. But you know? She's done pretty well over time."

Doc smiled. "You're right. And after the rheumatoid arthritis hit, we've seen what she's really made of. She's become an admirable woman."

At least I'd given her some measure of comfort. "Thanks, Doc. I appreciate all you've done for me."

"No problem, Haley girl. Just be careful you don't soak that hand for a couple of days. I want to see it again next Thursday. And if it gets hot or—"

"If the skin around the wound turns red or gets hot, I need to call you right away. You'll check it out, decide if it's infected or not, and prescribe an antibiotic if it is. I know the drill. Remember, Mom was a nurse."

"One of the best too." He handed me a prescription for a painkiller, even though we both knew I wouldn't fill it. "Just in case."

"See ya."

"Take better care of yourself, will you?"

"I'll try, Doc. I'll give it my best."

On the way home, I let Bella chatter. I offered an occasional "Uh-huh" and a couple of "No way!"s and that did the job. She was happy, and I got a chance to sift through the sludge in my head.

I wasn't the only one with tragedy in my past. And I had no more right to my pent-up rage than the next person did.

I was glad they'd made me see Tedd.

I don't do invalid. So while I channel surfed and found nothing to watch, my mind did overtime on what I'd learned so far. For the first time since the murder, something rivaled it for first place in my thoughts.

What had Gussie done? I couldn't see her as a bank robber, cat burglar, or jaywalker, for goodness' sake. What law had she broken?

No matter what loony scenario I cooked up, I couldn't fit her in the starring role. Except for one. One I didn't like.

I'd have to ask Dad about it, and even though he'd balk at discussing a parishioner's past, this could affect my future.

I've never been a patient woman, and today that failure made me nuts. What was keeping Dad so late at church? Well, he was actually five minutes late. I am impatient. When his steps finally sounded on the porch, I rushed to open the door.

"Haley!" He saw the massive gauze mitt Doc had lashed on me. "What happened?"

I'd almost forgotten my accident. "Oh, it's nothing. I cut myself with some scissors, and you know Doc. He went to town on the bandage thing."

Dad's eyes narrowed. "Yes, dear, I do know Doc. That looks a lot like something to me. How many stitches?"

Since I hadn't asked, I couldn't answer. "Dunno. Some, but it doesn't hurt." Much.

My father shook his head. "Is this why you felt the need to greet me like that?"

I blushed. "Ah . . . no."

How was I going to lead up to my questions without upsetting him again? After all, I'd done so spectacularly well with the stolen statue bit.

"I have to talk to you, and it's important. I've learned some things that might help clear me."

A frown lined his brow. "I don't like the sound of this."

"And you won't like my questions either, but I need the answers, Dad. I'm not kidding around."

"Okay, Haley. At least let me sit down." He took his favorite armchair, and I took Mom's rocker. "What's it about?"

"It's about Gussie, Dad." At his incredulous look, I hurried to add, "It's not some crazy idea. Gussie said something today, and then Doc added to it. They got me thinking."

"A dangerous proposition with you."

"Just tell me this. Did Gussie turn into a kleptomaniac after she miscarried?"

My father looked as though I'd punched him. "You know I can't break a parishioner's confidence. I'm Gussie's pastor."

"But you're my father, and I've a lot at stake."

"You think Gussie stole the statue."

"I don't know, but she could have."

"And if she did, what does it mean?"

"I don't know, Dad, but that statue gives me the willies. I can't tell you more, because that's all I know. I just have a strong feeling that Marge's murder and the statue are connected. I just don't know how."

"I've never done this, Haley. I'm only doing it because I'm afraid of what you might do to get your answer."

I went to argue, but he stopped me.

"You wanted my answer, didn't you?" When I nodded, he said, "Then, yes. Gussie stole little things here and there. People grew suspicious, but because she's such a favorite, they gave her the benefit of the doubt. Then she was caught with a quart of cooking oil from the supermarket. The owner agreed not to press charges if she got help."

"Cooking oil? That's crazy."

"No, it's typical. Kleptomaniacs don't steal out of need but from an inner hunger. What they take isn't the issue."

"So did she? Get help, I mean."

"Yes, she chose to meet with me rather than a psychologist." Dad averted his gaze. "She knew only God could help her heal."

His refusal to meet my gaze said more than a dictionary's worth of words could. He felt I should do the same, turn to God, but I wasn't Gussie, even though we both knew painful loss.

I stood and placed a hand on his shoulder. He looked up. Tears filled his eyes.

"Thanks, Dad," I choked out. Then I ran upstairs.

I didn't know what the new information meant.

"So stress can trigger kleptomania?" I said to Tedd three days later.

"That's the usual trigger, yes."

"Any particular kind of stress?"

"Not really. Anything can trigger it in a person who's predisposed."

"Tell me something else. Is it uncontrollable? Does the person realize what they're doing is wrong and can't help but steal? Or is the person so disturbed they no longer know right from wrong?"

Tedd sighed. "It's not black and white. The answer lies somewhere in the middle of all that. Most of the time, the patient knows it's wrong, but the inner void hurts so much that they go ahead and focus on the adrenaline rush that goes with the theft to avoid the pain."

"So Gussie would have known what she did was wrong."

"Probably. Anyone with any conscience will struggle with the compulsive aspect of kleptomania. In the end, though, they choose to commit the crime for the sake of the exhilaration that masks the pain for a while."

"But that means they'll wind up with a new kind of pain."

"We won't have to worry about kleptomania with you." Tedd grinned. "That's the difference between you and someone in the grip of that problem."

"You mean Dad's right when he says that all crime—sin is his preferred word—boils down to choice?"

"God's the one who said it. Your dad just repeated it."

"You don't give up, do you?"

"I'm not in the business of giving up."

"Okay, okay. I'm seeing a connection between Gussie's loss and her lousy choice. Maybe what I need is to find someone who blames a loss on Marge. Then I'll know who chose to kill her."

"That's one possibility."

"Then that would point to either Ozzie or Dutch. But I can't figure out how Dutch would blame Marge for the loss of his reputation."

"Okay . . ."

"I don't see where either Noreen or Steve would have blamed Marge for any loss. Neither lost anything until after she died."

"Unless Steve was trying to end things with Noreen."

"I don't think Noreen's that much in love with Steve."

"Love might not have anything to do with it. Love doesn't necessarily lead to possessiveness."

"But where would the statue come in if one of them did it?"

"Where does the statue come in with Ozzie? Or don't you think the statue's important anymore?"

I dropped my head back against the chair. "I don't know. Every time I learn something new, everything else gets muddier."

"Tell you what," Tedd said. I sat up, hungry for help. "Why don't you talk to Ozzie? I don't think you ever did."

"You're right. The offices were vandalized when I got there. I wonder if Karate Chop Cop found out who broke in."

"You might want to ask her."

I checked my watch. "Since my session's over, I think I'll head to the warehouse. And maybe I'll give the detective a call."

"Sounds like a plan." Tedd walked me to the door. "But be careful, Haley. This isn't a game."

A knot lodged in my throat. "I know, Tedd. I know too well."

But that seemed about all I really knew. Odd snippets floated in my thoughts, but there was nothing I could grab, nothing that gelled. I gave up trying to chase them and thought about the questions I had for Ozzie.

All I had to do, however, was mention the partnership to him. Ozzie answered like a broken dam.

"It simply wasn't fair, Miss . . . er . . . Haley. I made a mistake—one mistake fifteen years ago. All that time Marge held it over my head."

"That doesn't sound like Marge."

"Marge was many different women," Ozzie answered in an angry voice. "She could hold a grudge forever, and she did."

"Why don't you tell me what you did? I won't discuss it with anyone, but it's only fair that I know, since I'm supposed to be the new owner of all this."

Ozzie came out from behind his desk, his face pale, his expression strained. "You must understand what I was up against. My wife's cancer had advanced to where she suffered unbearable pain. I had to give her the best I could. And that kind of care cost more than I made working for Marge."

Was this about yet another bad choice?

He gestured toward the door that led to the warehouse. "I know a great deal about antiques. Anyone who does can doctor a piece to make it look authentic. The difference in price between a good replica and the real thing is astounding, and the work involved is minimal."

"Oh, Ozzie. You faked some pieces for the money."

"I'm not proud of it, but I also don't know that I would act differently given the same circumstances. My desperation in the face of Laura's suffering was more than I can describe."

"Marge could've fired you."

"I know." He grimaced. "It's a small consolation, since what she did is probably worse. She held my transgression over my head all these years. I couldn't seek a job elsewhere, because she would have revealed the forgeries in any recommendation she gave. At the same time, she refused me the trust that would have allowed me to move into partnership with her."

"Did you ever do it again?"

"Never."

His single word answer left no doubt. I believed him. And his anger, in his mind, was justified. Had it led him to murder? Was the memo the smoking gun?

"There's one more thing, Ozzie. Did you two argue about this the day of the Gerrity auction?"

"You want to know if I killed Marge for the business."

I blushed, but didn't reply.

His shoulders sagged. "What good would it do me? I had no illusions about her will. In fact, she told me she wrote a codicil about the forgeries. Her death means that sooner or later, my problems will become public."

He walked to the door, opened it, and looked toward the warehouse with longing. "I didn't expect you to inherit, but I knew I wouldn't. Now I risk unemployment. I'm in my late fifties and practically unemployable. Goodness knows I don't have the funds to buy this from you."

Okay. So motive? Eh . . . sort of.

Opportunity? The same.

Means? No better.

"When did you last see the Erté?"

"Ah . . . let me see . . . I unwrapped it at the Gerrity mansion that morning. I'd taken a box of the smalls with me and set them up when I got there."

"That was the last time, then?"

"Yes. At around seven o'clock."

"So anyone could have taken it after that."

"I suppose. But what does the bronze have to do with anything?"

"I don't know yet, Ozzie, but you can be sure I'm going to find out."

We went our separate ways after that. I detoured to Marge's office and saw the same mess I'd left behind. I don't know what made me go there, but maybe I needed to reconnect with the woman I once thought I knew so well.

I'd learned things about my mentor that made me question my judgment. But after some thought I realized I'd always seen her through the eyes of a girl. Marge had lived a life different from the one I'd seen. She'd had ugly spots in her past, ones she'd kept hidden.

She hadn't been a member of Dad's flock, but she'd often joined in church activities because of her friendships with many members, starting with my parents. I'd thought her a good person, and I suppose by most accounts that's how she'd be judged.

Ever since Tedd and I had talked about choices, sins, and crimes, I wondered if being a good person was enough. Had someone chosen to kill her because they didn't like her? That was stupid.

Or had Marge made choices in life that had led to someone's hate? Hate that eventually led someone to kill her. Was that what Dad and the others would see as Marge's greatest sin?

I'd have to think about that.

With a sigh, I started toward the door. I stepped on a wad of paper and stooped to pick it up. It was a bundle, held together with a wide rubber band. It looked like letters, and I couldn't resist a closer look.

The signature at the bottom of the letters chilled me to the bone. They were love letters, and they were signed, "Yours always, your Tom."

As if my head were a coin sorter, shards of information

clicked into various slots. If these letters were from Tom Stoker, then everything I knew now wore a different shade of threat. The dates coincided with what Dad and Doc had said about Gussie's miscarriage. Had both traumas hit Gussie at the same time? Had the affair added to the stress of losing her child? Was this what had pushed her beyond her conscience and into kleptomania?

A worse scenario occurred to me. Had Gussie found out about the affair, and the anguish led to the loss?

My heart pounded and my fingers shook as I dialed Doc Cowan's number. "Doc," I pleaded. "Please. This is important. It might mean the difference between a conviction and freedom for me."

"What is it, Haley? What are you talking about?"

"Remember when you sewed up my hand the other day?"

"Of course."

"Remember what you said about Gussie, her miscarriage, and her problems with the law?"

Silence. Then a reluctant, "Yes."

"I understand about all the confidentiality business, but this is about murder and jail. Please, Dr. Cowan, I have to know if there's a connection between the miscarriage, the kleptomania, and Tom's affair with Marge."

Doc's sigh told me all I wanted to know. But I waited for his confirmation. "Yes, Haley. Gussie found out about Tom's infidelity and couldn't handle it. She'd had a terrible pregnancy. Her emotions were very fragile. Then she went into labor, and Tom was nowhere to be found."

"Oh, please . . . don't tell me—"

"Your parents brought her to the hospital. Tom didn't show up until it was all over and the child was dead." Doc paused, then said, "He was in Marge's bed that whole time."

17

I sat for a long time in Marge's office chair. Doc's words rang in my ears; the knowledge shattered me. Tears drenched my cheeks, and I mourned the loss of my memories.

Nothing was as I'd thought.

If this was what being grown-up was all about, it stunk worse than I'd thought. Pity I couldn't go back.

Something tried to take shape in my thoughts, but the fear it brought made me fight it with a vengeance.

After a while I realized I couldn't stay any longer. I had things to do. More questions needed answers.

Plus, I had another special missionary society event that afternoon. A tea party, for goodness' sake. It struck me as even more ridiculous than before in view of all I'd learned. How was I going to act in front of Gussie? How was I going to act cheerful, chatty, and nice?

Three hours later I had to wonder if Dutch had seen something I didn't know I had in me. I was a bang-up actress. Everyone complimented me on how well I ran the tea, considering.

I was sick of that "considering" business. I wanted the whole mess to go away. But since it wasn't about to do that, I'd take whatever I could get. I wanted to run home, grab pen and paper, and make a list of all I knew. Maybe then, if I connected figurative dots, I'd understand.

Still, that looming fear held me back. Did I really want to know the truth? No matter how awful it might be?

"You betcha," I whispered. I needed to stay out of jail.

I looked around and saw that most of the women had left. Thank goodness. Then I realized who was still in the meeting room.

"I'm sick of hearing so much about the suddenly sainted Marge," Penny complained.

Ina gave Penny one of her careful, discreet smiles. "I'm sorry you feel that way, Penny, but please, do remember. The woman's dead."

"One wonders what she did *this* time to get her head bashed in." The way Penny said it made me cringe.

Ina walked away, shaking her head in obvious disgust. But Bella wasn't about to let Penny get away so easily.

"Look, Penny. If you know something, spill it. There's a murder investigation going on."

"Wouldn't you like to be the supersleuth," Penny countered. "But it doesn't take a genius to figure it out."

Bella grinned. "Sure doesn't."

Penny glared. "If all your Jessica Fletcher books and stuff make you so smart, how come you didn't figure out that Marge was running around with a married man again?"

"Sure she was." Bella crossed her rotund arms. "Her husband."

"Not at all. I saw her in downtown Seattle at one of those weird vegetarian, new-agey cafés with him. And it sure wasn't Steve I saw."

Dread slowed my approach. "Penny, you have to back up that kind of accusation with proof. Otherwise, it's just gossip."

"Oh, look who's acting all righteous. The seductress's heir."

I ground my teeth, counted to ten, tried again. "You can't insult a woman whose body hasn't even been released by the coroner yet. Who do you think Marge seduced?"

"I don't think. I saw them myself. She and Tom Stoker were sitting cozy as a pair of cooing turtledoves on stools at that place. And right in the front window, mind you."

I took a step back. It couldn't be true. "You'd better be sure about this. You don't know how much harm accusations like that can do."

Bella nodded. "Especially if it's not true. You could hurt a good marriage."

Penny shrugged. "I know what I saw. And I have excellent eyesight. You could always ask Tom. I bet he says I'm right."

I'd already decided to do that, but now came the hardest thing. "Please don't repeat this, even if you're sure. Gossip is rotten and dangerous."

"I don't care," the postal clerk said. "I know what I know. That's all I care about. Good night."

I was glad to see her go.

Bella harrumphed. She walked me to the door, waited until I locked up, then followed me home. "Think she'll keep that big fat mouth of hers shut?"

"Unfortunately, no."

"So what're we going to do?"

"*We're* not going to do anything, Bella. *We're* going home, making dinner, eating, and spending a quiet evening minding our business."

"But it *is* your business to find out if Marge was messing with Tom. Maybe Penny got it wrong. Maybe she saw Marge with a man but he only looked like Tom and that's who offed her."

My thoughts exactly, but I didn't want to encourage Bella. "Tell you what. How about I call the detective and tell her?"

Bella snorted. "What kind of sleuth are you, anyway? You have no gumption, and you're no fun. Am I gonna have to figure this out by myself?"

"No, Bella, neither one of us is going to do anything crazy. I'm going to do the smart thing and call the cops."

"Boooring!" With a toss of her bushy pink head, Bella marched home in a snit. As soon as her door slammed shut, I jumped in the Honda and pulled out. I wanted to waylay Tom before he got back from his daily round of golf.

I got to the clubhouse as he was unlocking the van door. "Tom! Wait a minute. Please!"

"Haley! Has something happened to Gussie?"

Great. He went right to the heart of it. I braced myself. "No, not that I know of. But she could be in for a nasty time."

"What do you mean?"

I really didn't want to do it. "I'll warn you. I have to ask some questions that won't be fun. Not for me to ask, nor for you to answer. But things could get worse if you don't."

Tom slipped his hands in his pockets. Tension radiated from his stiff shoulders to the tight line of his lips. "Go ahead. Let's get it over with."

"There's no easy way to do it, so I'm just going to ask. Were you having an affair with Marge again?"

He flinched. Color left his face. "A . . . gain?"

"I know what happened all those years ago. I know about the affair, about the miscarriage. I even know about the stealing. What matters now is whether you and Marge got back together again. Recently, that is."

"I can't believe it's come back to haunt me again." Defeat and grief marked his face. "I made a horrible mistake fifteen years ago, and it cost Gussie and me the greatest treasure we could have had. We lost our son because of what I did. Just think what life is like with that in your heart."

His eyes glittered with unshed tears. "I've lived with that knowledge and shame ever since. Nothing on earth could entice me to stray again. I love Gussie. I always did."

"Then what about Marge—"

"Some men make fools of themselves when their wives are pregnant. I had a hard time with the loss of Gussie's undivided attention. Marge offered what I thought I needed. It was wrong—*I* was wrong, and my stupidity cost the life of a child."

"So you didn't go to some café in Seattle with Marge?"

"Someone saw us?"

"You did!"

"Yes. We met to discuss a business arrangement. You know that I do a great deal of woodworking now that I'm retired, don't you?"

"I've seen the beautiful pieces you make for Gussie."

"Thanks. Anyway, Marge had customers who wanted someone to restore antiques without affecting their value. She offered to refer clients my way. We first met with a client and were still hammering out details to the agreement at the café."

"So you hadn't resumed the affair?"

"No, Haley. I'm no fool. I can get you a copy of the contract Marge and I signed."

"You better show it to Gussie before the gossips get to her."

He nodded. "I hope you understand why I didn't want her to know. But I have nothing to hide this time. Let me hurry home and talk to her. Who knows how long I have before the buzz heats up."

I watched him drive away. On the one hand, I was glad that Marge hadn't repeated her earlier mistake. On the other hand, I no longer held out hope for a tolerable perp.

Again that hint of fear hovered in the back of my mind. I pushed it aside and grabbed my cell phone.

"Hey, Tedd. You wouldn't have a free minute this afternoon, would you?"

"Sure. I'm done with my last client. I was about to go through my notes from the day's sessions, but I'm available. Are you okay?"

"I think so, but I'm confused. And it seems that talking to you helps me sort through my sludge."

"Prayer would do more."

"Not now. Please." The comfort I once knew in my faith tugged at me, but I had more questions and doubts than answers in that regard. "I need to talk. Want to meet for dinner?"

"That's a great idea. Where do you want to go?"

"It's gotta be cheap—I'm broke, you know."

"Mickey Dee's will do, if you don't mind."

"I can afford that. See you down at the one on Breezewalk and Pine."

Fifteen minutes later we carried our trays to a booth. As if by mutual accord, we dug into our food and talked about nothing much. But once we'd finished our fries, Tedd gave me one of her penetrating looks.

"Spill it."

"I'm having a hard time with all the crud I've mucked up about people I like. They're not who I thought they were."

She smiled. "So you've realized they're human too, full of warts and wrinkles and secrets and lies."

"Something like that."

"Why are you having trouble with reality?"

I didn't know how to get around it, so I just let 'er rip. "Because it looks like anyone is capable of murder—for real, not just a cliché. Anyone could have killed Marge."

"Welcome to the real world, Haley. People are fallen sinners, like Scripture says, and only by the grace of God do we have any hope at all."

I felt the reflexive urge to silence the mention of God, but I couldn't go through with it this time. I was torn two ways; I wanted the comfort of the faith I had once known, but I also wanted to scream at the God who allowed evil and sin.

"I guess there's something to this deal with Tom and Marge," I ventured. "They had an affair years ago. That's what really caused Gussie's miscarriage. It seems they recently agreed for Tom to do restorations for Marge's clients. Someone saw them together in Seattle."

"They jumped to the obvious conclusion."

"Yes, Penny's great at leaping in the wrong direction."

"And what does that have to do with you?"

"That's what I don't know yet." I sighed. "I guess what I'm trying to say is that if someone is predisposed to suspect Tom, then seeing him with Marge would do it for sure."

"Sounds good so far."

"No, it's bad. It's another case of those bad choices we talked about that other time."

"You mean sin."

"If that's what you want to call it."

"I call it what it is, Haley. It'd be good if you did too."

"Anyway, it probably was a bad idea for Tom to work with Marge, in view of their past history."

"I see where you're going with this, and I agree. I also see that you don't want to go there, no matter how possible it seems."

"Do you blame me?" Anger sparked. "I've lost so much. First Paul did a number on me. Then Mom died, then Marge, and now I'm about to lose—"

I stopped myself. I couldn't say it. I just couldn't.

"What were you going to say, Haley?"

"What I want to know is what kind of God abandons someone he loves like he abandoned me? I only have Dad now, and he's not young anymore. I can't drag him into my problems. I'm alone, Tedd. All alone."

The rage made my cry guttural, and I saw a mom pull her

little girl closer. I gave her an apologetic smile, but I knew what I felt.

"So tell me, Tedd. Where's God? Where's the comfort and presence he's supposed to offer?"

Tedd reached across the table and covered my fist. "He's here, Haley. He's everywhere you've been."

"Then why doesn't he *do* something to stop all this? Why doesn't he help me? Why'd he leave me to rot and hurt all on my own?"

"You're not alone, you know. You have your dad, you have Tyler, and I'd like to think you know that you have me too."

"That's not what I meant—"

"Listen to me, will you?" When I nodded, she continued. "You were arrested, weren't you?"

I nodded.

"Are you still in jail?"

"No, but—"

"How'd you get out, Haley? Did the cops just open up the cell and tell you to head on home by bedtime?"

"No, Dad—"

"Aha! Your father came to help, didn't he? And his wasn't the only help, was it?"

"Yes . . . no . . . I don't know what you're getting at."

"Give me a chance." She patted my hand, then slipped a glossy lock of black hair behind an ear. "Your father wasn't about to let you rot in jail. What makes you think your heavenly Father, who loves you and your dad way more than you love each other, has abandoned you? Didn't he provide the money for your father to make bail? Didn't he provide the doctor who put you back together years ago after Paul tore you to shreds? Didn't God urge Tyler, your dad, and even Gussie to make you come see me?"

The tears fell on the tabletop. I couldn't speak.

Tedd had no such problem. "Haley, God's been by you the whole time. You closed him out, and that's where the pain comes from. Let him in. He's knocking at your heart's door. Would you shut your earthly father out like that?"

I shook my head. Sobs hitched my breath.

"Reach out and grab what the Lord's giving you."

"I don't know . . . what's he giving me, Tedd?"

"He's giving you life, a restored life where healing is total and his love is irresistible. But you have to let him in."

"I . . ." A sob cracked my voice. "I don't know how."

"Take that first step. Just say yes."

I surprised even myself. I whispered, "Yes."

18

Something in me shifted in that McDonald's booth. I didn't feel better after Tedd and I said good-bye; I just knew I was a different woman from the one who had called her therapist and asked to meet at a fast-food place.

I'd never heard of a shrink who hit the Golden Arches with a client. But nothing about my life had been normal for a long time now. So why should I expect Tedd to be typical?

I was changing. But I had no control over the change. I had to wonder if Dad and Tyler had been right all along. They'd said that God wouldn't quit chasing me until I let him catch me again.

Was that what I'd just done?

Back home, I pulled out my portfolio and played for a while with the placement of decorative accents in Gussie's living and dining rooms.

I'd talked Gussie into storing a number of her tchotchkes, and the ones we chose to use would add just the right touch to the new décor. I spread out the photos I'd taken and began to group items by size and color on a list. Then I divided them into potential groupings on specific pieces of furniture.

When I got to the table by the window I'd draped with the Thai silk, I stopped. I checked the photo and realized I hadn't imagined a thing. The Erté wasn't in the picture. It wasn't something the Stokers had owned for any length of time. It had appeared after my visit, days after Marge's death.

But it had been on the auction list.

My heart began to pound. Too many coincidences led back to that house, that statue, that couple.

It wasn't what I wanted, but I had no control.

In a flash, I saw what Tedd had tried to tell me. What Dad and Mom and Tyler had also said. I didn't have control over what anyone else did. And while God could control anything and everything, he had given his creation the freedom to choose. God could intervene, but then he'd be no more than a master puppeteer.

A puppet couldn't love back. And that was what God asked. His children had to choose whether they'd love him enough to obey or whether they'd go the other way.

I had to accept that God gave everyone the same freedom.

I didn't know how I was going to make it through the next few hours, days, alone. But if Tedd was right, I didn't have to. In a hesitant voice, I said, "God . . . if you're listening . . . help me, please."

I was amazed by how easy it was to turn to a life of crime. True, I did it for a good cause, to save my skin, but I stole something. Something major, at that.

Gussie went to bed at nine o'clock most nights. She said the pain drained her and she needed that much sleep to function the next day. I called and told her I needed a couple more measurements but that I couldn't make it over until closer to nine thirty.

"That's fine, Haley. Tom's a night owl. He'll be up until at least midnight. I'll let him know you're coming."

True to her word, she'd told Tom about my visit. He let me in, told me to make myself at home. "I'm working on my miniature train set in the basement," he said. "I won't get in your way."

I couldn't believe how easy it was. I hurried to the living room, walked around the room to make sure Tom heard and didn't get suspicious. I grabbed the statue and stuffed it into my roomy backpack purse.

"Hey, Tom! I'm done. I'll be on my way—"

"Hold on," he said. "I'd like a minute with you."

That's when I started to sweat. Had he figured out I was up to no good? Well, no good in terms of the statue, but good for the sake of my skin.

"What's up?" I asked when he joined me by the front door.

"I wanted to tell you I didn't get a chance to talk to Gussie yet. You know, about Marge."

"What can I say? I don't think you have much time. Penny's not known for her discretion."

"So it's Penny. I am in trouble. As soon as Gussie's over this latest spell, I'll make sure to tell her. As it is, you're the only person she's spoken to besides me. Maybe I can keep it that way until she's better."

"Good luck."

Not only would he need luck to keep the effects of Penny's wicked tongue at bay, but I'd need some good fortune as well. I was headed to the cop shop.

Once I was sure what I wanted to do, I called Tyler. He asked why I cared about Detective Tsu's schedule, and I asked him to give me space. He wasn't happy about it, but he said she'd left the *dojo* after her eight o'clock class. She'd planned to go to the station, since she'd said she had paperwork to catch up on.

This time, I didn't bear down through the halls of justice like a drill bit through soft pine but instead did the regulation bit. I told the dispatcher I had to see Detective Tsu, that it was urgent.

The woman who came out to meet me looked nothing like the one I knew, not the ultraelegant professional or the dedicated martial arts student either. Detective Tsu wore a pair of gently faded jeans that fit her to perfection and a T-shirt in an attractive shade of gold, and her hair hung loose to her shoulder blades. She looked like any other woman. True, not many looked quite that gorgeous, but tonight the air of intimidating perfection I'd come to associate with her wasn't there.

"This is a strange time to stop by the department," she said.

"I have to talk to you."

"So I gather."

Her up-and-down inspection made me aware of how I must look—tired, hair as wild as ever, and clothes more wrinkled than not. Still, I refused to let her intimidate me.

"Let's go to my office," she finally said. "We can talk there."

I followed in silence, preparing what I'd say. But as was usually the case, the minute the door closed, all my planned eloquence joined the cow and jumped over the moon. I blurted everything out.

"So here's the statue," I said at the end of my monologue.

"I'm afraid my fingerprints are everywhere, but maybe you can test for others too."

She shook her head. "You think this is necessary?"

"I don't think it's necessary, I *know* you have to test this thing. I've told you about the Stokers, and now I have photos with dates on the prints. Something's up with this thing."

I plunked the bronze on her immaculate desk. The dark stain at the base of the statue caught my eye again. A grotesque possibility occurred to me. "I just remembered something I noticed the first time I saw this. Do you see that stuff down there?"

The detective nodded without much interest.

"At first I thought it was a matter of age. You know, patina." I waited for Detective Tsu's nod. "Now I'm not so sure. It's only in one spot, and it doesn't look like a stain as much as something encrusted in the folds of the dress."

Just thinking about it made me sick.

Detective Tsu picked up the Erté. She looked it over, turned it around, then ran a short, rose-polished nail over the stain. She stiffened, then shot a look my way.

"You might be right about one thing," she said. "This could be encrusted matter and not a mark of age."

Even though her words did nothing for my twitchy stomach, I felt vindicated. "So you'll test the bronze?"

"You've left me with no alternative, have you?" Karate Chop Cop didn't sound happy about it, but grudging admiration showed in her face. "Still, how do you explain the bloody rock? It was Marge's blood—your fingerprints too."

"I don't know. Maybe when she fell she struck her head on the rock. You know, the wound itself."

"Maybe . . . You realize that if this turns out to be significant, then I'll owe you an apology. You stuck to your guns, and you might have come up with something."

"Someone had to do it."

Detective Tsu conceded with grace. "And you thought I wasn't doing it."

"Opinion nothing. You did nothing but look for ways to tie me to the crime."

"I'm sorry that's the impression you have of my investigation. Believe me, I did more than pursue you." She placed the statue on the desk. "It'll take a day or two to get anything back from the lab. Please don't do anything crazy before I call you with results."

"I'll try." Something else came to mind. "Will you release Marge's body for burial now?"

"It's not up to me, but I think the coroner's been done for days. Her next of kin, her husband, hasn't claimed her body yet."

"He's a pig," I muttered. "I'll speak to Dad about it. He'll call you to make arrangements."

She nodded. "By the way, and just so you know, we caught the kids who vandalized the warehouse. They've been very thorough in that area. I don't think there's a building they haven't hit in one way or another."

I shrugged. "That's good."

Karate Chop Cop sent me a crooked grin. "Yes, it is. In more ways than one. As is our discovery of Marge's Rolodex. It was under another rhododendron, covered with a thin layer of mulch."

"Really?"

"Yes, really. Interestingly enough, the entire *S* section was missing.

I winced. "It makes sense, even though it doesn't make me any happier."

"I understand." The detective then glanced at the running computer.

I got the hint. "I won't keep you any longer, but please let me know what you find out. I know I'm still your prime suspect, but I can't go on like this much longer."

For good measure, I added, "I didn't kill Marge."

Without making promises, Detective Tsu agreed that mine was a terrible position.

At the door, I paused. "That's the understatement of the century."

I left, and although I should have felt somewhat better, I dreaded the lab results. Either way, Marge was still dead.

"Haley, honey," Gussie said the next morning. "I just had to call. I'm so sorry I missed you last night, but you know how the morphine knocks me out when the pain gets really bad."

I'd had a moment of panic when I heard her voice. "That's okay. I did what I had to do and didn't stay long. I've been busy these last few days."

"How much more do you have to do to finish the rooms?"

"Not much. I have to bring over some accessories and lamps I picked up. The upholsterer delivered the couch and chair, didn't she?"

"And they look wonderful! You have such an excellent eye. Tell you what. Why don't you and the reverend come to dinner tonight? That way you can bring the accessories, and we can celebrate a job well done."

There was no getting around it. "That sounds great. What time?"

"Around six, as usual. And I'll make those turkey tenderloins you like so well."

"Just don't go to any trouble. You haven't been feeling well, and you don't want to make things worse."

"Don't worry. After all these years, I know what I'm doing."

"I'll see you later, then."

"Good-bye."

I was pretty sure I knew what had happened to Marge, but knowing didn't make me any happier. I hoped the lab did their thing fast so Detective Tsu could wrap things up. For the first time in a long time, I wanted to get on with my life, find out what God had in store for me, since it looked like he'd snuck up and caught me, as Tyler had predicted he would.

I wasn't there yet, but I had taken a couple of baby steps.

"Dinner was wonderful, as always, Gussie," Dad said, all smiles.

She smiled. "You're welcome. As always."

"Well, Reverend," Tom said, standing. "Gussie tells me she and Haley have a bunch of knickknacks they want to play around with. I don't know about you, but that's not my kind of thing. Want to run down to the driving range for a bucket of balls?"

Dad and Tom had little in common. Tom was a jock, a fan

of all things golf. Dad was an intellectual, more comfortable with books than with golf clubs and balls. But he was a good sport.

He shrugged. "Can't say I'll hit many, but I'm willing to try my hand at it. Just don't expect much." He turned to me. "I'll drive home after the golf, since you have your car."

Hmm . . . I didn't like this. "How about you stop by here? I'm taking the old coffee table and can't handle it alone."

Dad gave me a weird look but agreed to my request.

Thank goodness.

The two men left, and anxiety came. I hadn't known how to hold them back without making a fuss, but I didn't like the sudden silence in the house.

"Shall we start?" Gussie asked, her eyes bright, maybe too bright.

"No time like the present." I wanted nothing more than to finish so I could go home. "I left the box in the living room when we got here. Let's start there."

Things went well in that room. It wasn't until we got to the dining room that I noticed the feverish light in Gussie's eyes.

My stomach sank.

"I have to thank you for the fine job you've done on our home." Gussie's voice came out sharp and excited. "You've taken good care of me, and it's only right that I take care of you now."

That was all I needed.

"I'm fine, Gussie. I take pretty good care of myself. Remember what you told Bella. I've been studying martial arts for a while now."

She waved. "That's not the kind of care you need, honey.

I have to make sure they don't lock you up in that horrible jail again. I know how to do it too."

Gussie spoke fast, seemingly propelled by some powerful force. I wondered how much medication she'd taken, if it had affected her more than usual. If that was what made me fear her so much.

"I can't let you suffer," she added. "I have a plan."

"A plan?"

"Everything's ready." She pointed to the table, where a pen lay on some sheets of paper. "You just have to write your friend the detective a nice note, and then I'll give you something to soothe you, something that'll help you get the rest you need. You've been working too hard, you know."

Gee, how nifty. The woman who was about to kill me was worried about my rest . . . or lack thereof.

"I'm fine. I loved doing your rooms. And now I can't wait to start on Noreen's new house. She wants to buy the Gerrity, you know."

Gussie frowned. "I'm sorry. Noreen's going to have to find herself another designer. You need your rest. And I can't go to jail, you know. It's just not possible."

At least she knew the consequences of what she'd done. "Gussie, no one's going to put you in jail. Just talk to Detective Tsu. She's a very understanding woman."

Yeah, right. But at this point, I'd say just about anything to save my hide. How had I wound up like this? All I'd wanted was justice for Marge and to stay out of jail.

"You know that won't work, Haley," Gussie said. "She's not an understanding woman. Look how she nearly got you convicted of a crime you didn't commit."

As Mom used to say, in for a penny, in for a pound. "A crime you committed, right, Gussie?"

She puzzled. "It's not a crime. I had to right an old wrong and keep the same thing from happening again. You understand. After all, it's a matter of justice."

"Justice or vengeance?"

"Oh, no! 'Vengeance is mine,' sayeth the Lord."

That's when I realized how bad things were. Gussie had lost touch with reality. Just as stress had once led her to steal, her damaged mind had made her exact vengeance in the form of murder.

"But I don't understand where I come in," I said. I hoped I could keep her talking long enough for Dad and Tom to finish their buckets of balls.

"Well, dear, things have changed now. I can't have you go to jail for Marge's untimely death. That wouldn't be right. And I do have to take care of you, now that your dear mother is gone. You're tired, honey. You need your rest."

"I'm really fine—"

"Please take a seat at the table, Haley." Although Gussie spoke with her usual gentleness, the gun in her hand spoke otherwise.

I sat.

"Where'd you get that?" What was I, crazy like Gussie? Who cared where the gun came from? "Why are you doing this?"

"Never mind the gun, Haley, and I'm not doing anything, dear. You're writing a note to your detective friend. Please make sure you tell her how sorry you are about Marge's murder. Oh, and don't forget to tell her you helped yourself to my morphine. It does help you get some lovely, lovely sleep."

Gussie's voice now rang brittle and reedy. She spoke fast, and that wild light in her eyes scared me more each minute.

"But—"

"Now, honey, you know it's not nice to argue with Mama. Do as I say, Haley. Everything will be fine." She motored over and reached for the cake stand in the middle of the table. "Here. I made some of that mocha torte you like so much. I have a pot of tea too."

Gussie sliced a wedge of cake. She handed me the plate, and a morbid chuckle almost slipped out. Coffee-flavored cake was going to be my last meal. Unfortunately, Gussie was going to make me wash it down with tea. I would have preferred Starbucks.

"Thanks," I said. My sarcasm went right over her head.

"See?" She smiled her old smile, and for a moment, tears filled my eyes. Another loss.

Then she added, "Mama knows best, Haley. Here's your tea now. And make sure you drink every drop. Mama put your bedtime tonic in it."

Horror surged in a rush of nausea, but I couldn't give up. I had to get through this. I had to outthink a woman who had truly lost her mind.

"Go ahead, Haley. Write that letter like a good girl."

The gun aimed for my head and never wavered. I took up the pen and wrote a confession to a murder I didn't commit.

"That's much better, dear. Now, eat your cake while you write. It's past your bedtime, and as soon as you're done, you'll have to go night-night."

I couldn't give panic a foothold. If I did, I was lost. I wrote and nibbled, nibbled some more. Finally, the cake was gone and the letter written.

"I'm off to bed now," I said, rising. I could move faster than Gussie. But I didn't know how good and fast she'd be with the gun. I didn't want to find out the hard way.

"The tea, dear." She clicked the gun's safety.

She wasn't that far gone. She knew I was a threat, and she knew she had to eliminate me. If I did it right, I could swig down enough of the laced tea and jump her. Once I had the gun, I'd just let my jumpy stomach do its thing. I was nervous enough that nausea wasn't a problem.

I sipped and grimaced. It tasted bitter, almost as bitter as the knowledge of what had happened to Marge. Gussie must have realized that Marge and Tom had been in contact. They'd only done business, but she must have assumed, based on past experience, that they'd been up to the old affair again.

She'd snapped. Plain and simple. Hatred like she'd carried for so many years had poisoned her just as the morphine was going to poison me.

I remembered what Tedd had said. I sure felt alone right now, but I prayed. For the first time in four-plus years, I called out to the God she insisted was at my side. I'm not sure if I did it in faith or desperation, but I knew he held the answer right then. I couldn't save myself.

But I was going to give it a good try.

"Drink up, Haley. It's getting late. You must be in bed before Papa gets home."

I swigged the rest of the foul mess in a couple of gulps, hoping my stomach would rebel.

It didn't.

"That's my good girl," Gussie said with a smile. "Now take your note, and let's go lie down in the lovely living room you made for me."

In that fraction of a second when she glanced at the wheelchair controls, I grabbed the silver Georgian epergne and hefted it at her gun hand. The heavy piece clipped the inflamed wrist. Gussie cried out in pain.

The weapon flew to the side. I dove after it. Gussie went for it too, but the arthritis held her back. I reached the gun first.

"Don't do it!" Gussie wailed.

I aimed, just to keep her from moving. I knew I'd never use the gun. But then the morphine hit.

The meltdown began in my legs. Before I knew what had happened, I lay on the Aubusson rug I'd ordered. "Hel . . . help!"

Men rushed in, their movements a weird blur. I heard them talk of cops and ambulances, but nothing made sense. I heard a pained keening, not a human sound, but I knew it came from a human, one tortured beyond the point of sanity.

A woman spoke.

Another cried, argued, roared.

A man yelled, "No!"

Another came and gathered me up in his arms. Everything spun. My stomach heaved; I retched. The last thing I saw was a pair of bright green eyes.

Epilogue

How many women throw up at the sight of a green-eyed white knight?

I know only one.

Me.

Poor Dutch—I couldn't believe I thought of him that way now. But he'd only wanted to help. And Bella, bless her nutty heart, after she watched me drive off, worried that I'd gone alone. She could have called Lila and her Smurfs, but instead, in true former-starlet form, she called the good-looking guy.

The cavalry drove up in a battered truck only to find me sprawled on the floor, doped on morphine, Gussie with a mohair throw in one hand and a gun in the other.

As Dutch and Bella burst in the door, Dad and Tom drove up. The noise startled Gussie, Bella snatched the gun, and Dutch picked me up. I threw up.

At least I didn't do it on him.

Gussie broke down, her wails haunting. When she saw Tom, however, she opened a vial of morphine. Tom cried, tried to wrestle it from her, but she'd worked herself up to a frenzy that gave her greater strength. She downed the whole thing.

Detective Tsu showed up then, ready to arrest Gussie. The initial test on the sculpture showed blood. By the time the ambulance arrived, there was nothing left to do. The morphine had done its job.

Lucky for me, or as Dad and Tedd would say, by the grace of God, my nervous stomach did its thing too. I only spent one night in the hospital.

I recovered quickly. Swallowing my distaste, I met again with Marge's lawyer—I refused to claim him in any way—and made some decisions about my bequest. The first was to give Steve a settlement and send the cheat on his way.

Then I did something that really felt right. I called Ozzie.

"I need your help," I told him.

"What kind?"

"Well, I seem to recall that Marge said you'd taught her how to do that crazy auction talk. Wanna teach me?"

He was silent for a beat. Then, "Of course. Does that mean you'll be taking over the business?"

"Only part of it."

He gasped. "What part . . . what does that mean . . . what's on your mind?"

"I know next to nothing about the antiques and auctions business, Ozzie. I think I'd better get a partner. Know any good ones?"

This time, the silence lasted forever . . . almost. "Come on, Ozzie. Aren't you going to answer?"

"Miss . . . er . . . Haley? Are you saying what I think you're saying?"

"Just so you know, Ozzie. I can't think of a better man to work with, to learn from, or to have as my right hand. Do you still want that share of the business? I figure your expertise is worth at least half."

His voice shook with emotion. "You won't regret it. I promise. You won't—"

"Thanks, Ozzie. I know I can trust you."

Dad walked into the kitchen as I wiped away the tears. I still had the phone in my hand.

"Who was that?"

When I told him what I'd done, he smiled. "You're getting there, Haley. I'm proud of you."

I shrugged. "It looks like you were right—you and Mom and Tyler and Tedd. God's poked a great big hole in my shell."

It was his turn for tears, quiet, deep-felt ones.

"I'm not there yet, Dad. But I think I'm on my way."

His gray eyes, so much like mine that I felt as though I'd looked in a mirror, spoke of love. "Remember, Haley. God will never let you down. 'He who began a good work in you—'"

"—will carry it on to completion until the day of Christ Jesus." I smiled. "I'm counting on him."

Two wild months later, I had reason to remember that little exchange with Dad. Oh, I'd done my part. I'd continued my sessions with Tedd, and we were well on the way to becoming friends. More and more we turned to Scripture during our sessions.

I was seeing my faith in a different light.

And I hadn't missed a chance to listen to my father present the Word of God in church. I'd even begun to enjoy the missionary society meetings—heaven help me.

But it was at the rescheduled auction of the Gerrity mansion that I really had to call on my new, baby-food faith.

Ozzie handled the whole thing with grace and his usual skill. I wasn't ready to try out my new chatter yet, certainly not on something as huge as the sale of a landmark.

So I sat in the audience and noticed Noreen at my side only when her paddle was the last to flash after the price reached Alpine heights.

"So," the socialite said once Ozzie accepted her final bid, "are you still going to do my new house? I mean, now that you're so busy with the business and don't need the money . . . are you still interested?"

"Yes, Haley." That certain contractor who knew more about my weaknesses than I cared to share butted in. "Are you going to make my life a nightmare with your ideas for furniture placement, froufrous, and paint?"

I looked at Dutch, then at Noreen. Could I work with them?

When I'd suspected anyone and everyone of killing Marge, and especially after I'd learned of Noreen's affair with Steve, I'd doubted I could go through with the project. But since then, I'd changed. I wasn't the same woman Marge had recommended.

Dutch shifted in his chair. I glanced at him, and his green gaze met mine. I blushed, the memory of the night Gussie tried to kill me too vivid to forget.

He'd driven me crazy, and we'd argued like cats. He was

cocky and arrogant, and he had a lousy reputation, but he'd saved my life.

I sighed, disgusted, but not sure at what.

Maybe God would grant me an extra measure of grace. He'd helped me with Gussie, and maybe now, with a different kind of help, he'd help me work with Dutch.

"Yeah." I smiled. "When do we start?"

Decorating Schemes

Coming in March 2006

Excerpt from
Decorating Schemes

Stripping is not the best way for a woman to earn her living. I mean, really. To start out with, the clothes you have to wear are nothing to write home about, and then look at what it does to your skin. All those caustic chemicals ruin your hands, you know? At least I'm the kind who wouldn't be caught dead at a nail salon; the cost of manicure upkeep would rival the federal deficit.

As an interior designer—not to mention the new owner, thanks to an inheritance—of a major auction house, I come in contact with more than my share of old pieces that need nips and tweaks, if not complete face-lifts. For that, I have to rely on those nasty stripping compounds. And don't even think about the all-natural or organic kind. They just don't do the job as well or as fast.

That leads me to the other problem. No matter what kind of gloves I use, they always wind up melted before I complete the fix to the furniture's finish. That's what my newest pair had started to do when the phone rang in the workshop at the warehouse.

"Norwalk Auctions, Haley Farrell speaking."

"Hi, Haley." The fudgy voice was more than familiar. Before I could respond to my latest—and first to live through the experience—design client, Noreen Daventry continued. "I hope I didn't catch you at a bad time."

For my gooey gloves, and the phone, no time would be good. The gloves were done for, and I'd have to douse the receiver with stripper to rid it of the rubbery mess, then hope and pray that kind of plastic wouldn't succumb to the chemical too. But I couldn't tell one of the richest women on the West Coast that I was too busy to talk to her.

"It's never a bad time for a chat with you, Noreen."

"That's very kind, Haley." A hint of humor underscored Noreen's voice, a clear reminder that we both knew more about each other than either of us would like.

"Since," she went on, "you're in such a benevolent mood, this should be a good time to ask you for a favor."

Groan. "Sure. What do you need?"

"I don't need anything. But I do have friends whose home is in dire need of your talents."

Now she was playing my kind of tune. "Really? What's their problem?"

"Oh, no problem. Just a house that hasn't been touched in the last . . . oh, I guess it must be fifteen years now. They're newlyweds, and Dr. Marshall would like to offer his darling new bride the chance to make the house hers."

"Dr. Marshall . . . do you mean Stewart Marshall, the plastic surgeon?"

"You know Stew, then."

"No, but I do read newspapers."

Noreen chuckled. "Then you already know this job would be very lucrative for you. And I've raved about your work to Deedee—the new Mrs. Marshall. They'd like you to come over as soon as possible—this evening, even—to take a good look at their place and give them your expert opinion. They like what you did with my new home."

Noreen bought a white-elephant money pit almost a year

ago at the first auction I ran after my inheritance cleared probate. I worked like a horse to finish the redesign in time for
her to move in this spring. She's been in the home a mere
eight weeks now and has already hosted six social-column-
worthy bashes.

"I'm glad." I checked every surface for paper and pen or
pencil but found none. Besides, my hands were in no condition
to touch anything. "Tell you what. I . . . ah . . . have a minor
mess to clear up here, and then I'll call you back."

A throaty laugh flowed over the connection. "Hope you're
not in trouble with the law again."

The nerve of the woman! I haven't been in trouble with
the law.

Never.

Not really.

They just jumped to judgment a few months back and
thought I'd committed a crime that anyone with a shred of
brain matter would know I never could have committed. But
I had to hold my tongue if I wanted to land the job—not a
piece of cake for me.

"Umm . . . er . . . no. Nothing like that. I just need to take care
of some ah . . . paperwork—" paper towels might do the job
. . . maybe "—to give the Marshalls my complete attention."

Another chuckle tested my patience, so I sent a quick prayer
heavenward.

"I'll be waiting for your call, then," Noreen said. "Oh, and
by the way. You might as well know ahead of time. The Marshalls decided to hire Dutch too."

This time I couldn't keep the groan to myself.

Noreen laughed harder. "That's what I thought. I suppose

I should warn Deedee that fireworks will be a daily thing when her general contractor and interior designer come face-to-face."

What could I say? Dutch Merrill and I don't see eye to eye on much. Actually, we don't see eye to eye on anything, as we discovered during the months we were forced to work together on Noreen's remodel.

True, we got off to a bad start. I knew he'd taken up more than his fair share of newsprint in the couple of years before we met; negligence and shoddy business practices were alleged. His acquittal in a court of law, however, hasn't done much to clear his name in the court of public opinion even now. The idea of my businesses associated with his doesn't exactly thrill me.

Even if his work at Noreen's place was outstanding.

A tantrum wouldn't do; I had to get a grip.

I had no choice but to play nice. "We did do a good job on the Gerrity mansion. You haven't stopped raving about your new home, and the Wilmont Historical Society feels that although we didn't necessarily restore the mansion to its original glory, we didn't hurt its architectural or historical integrity either."

"You've a point there. Even if you did fight like cats and dogs the whole time, you and Dutch somehow worked a miracle. The house looks fabulous, you both came in under budget, and you even finished three weeks ahead of schedule." She paused. Then, "But you have to admit, your spats did add a much-needed element of comic relief to a dreary process."

Oh, yeah. A woman always likes to hear she's become entertainment fodder for the obscenely wealthy. Dignity, Haley. Shoot for dignity.

"Don't worry, Noreen. Dutch and I can work just as well for the Marshalls as we did for you. Now, if you don't mind, I do have to get back to this mess—I mean, to the matter I have to clear up."

With still more of Noreen's laughter ringing in my ear, I ran to the bathroom next to the office in the warehouse, scraped the mushy remains of rubber gloves off my hands, and made use of my favorite bank-busting but essential moisture cleanser. The thick, creamy lather soothed my itchy hands, and the lukewarm water felt like a balm. The expensive scent? Well, it just smells good.

Was I ready to face off against Dutch Merrill again?

His handsome image materialized in my head. Yeah, he's a hunk, and he can fix a crumbled wall five hundred ways to Sunday, but his questionable reputation still cloaks him like green stuff on month-old leftovers. Then there's that embarrassing moment we shared a year ago.

"Aaargh!" The mere memory of that humiliating episode made me squeeze the tube of super-duper mega moisture with a hair more oomph than necessary.

"How long is it going to hover in the back of my mind, Lord?" As I wiped up goo and waited for a heavenly response, I spied my cowardly gray eyes in the mirror.

Bummer. Time to confess. "Okay, Father God. You're right. It'll hover as long as I keep dredging it up, as long as I take it back from where I dumped it at the foot of your Son's cross. But please cut me some slack. I'm still rusty at this faith thing, you know."

I've learned that faith isn't as easy as one—I—would like it to be. Once, I trusted with the sweet innocence of a pastor's child who heard and saw only the good side of the world. Then, as a young adult, my world crashed down on me thanks to a brutal, godless thug.

When, in the aftermath of that attack, the criminal justice system failed me, I turned away from the God I believed had also failed me. It's only now, after almost five years of hard-won progress and no more than partial healing, that I realize my almighty Father was always there at my side. I also know that I have a ways to go before trust and faith become the easy default setting for my gun-shy gray matter.

I turned from the mirror, hairbrush in hand. Blessed with a mane of uncivilized hair, the frequent application of brush to locks is required. I yanked and muttered on my way to the desk, hoping the prayer sank in, if by no other means than through the pores on my stinging scalp.

"Good grief, Haley Farrell." Maybe the lecture would give my attitude a healthy adjustment. "You're an interior designer with an insanely successful auction house on the side, not a bottom-sucking catfish. You have a job to do, and your job description does not include mental muck dredging—"

"Dredging, Miss Haley?"

"Aack!" I jumped a bazillion miles. "Ozzie! You scared the stuffing out of me. You're done already? When'd you get back?"

My partner, the meek, mild, and mousy Oswald "Ozzie" Krieger, stood in the open doorway to the bathroom, the usual frown on his basset-hound face. He'd gone to appraise an estate early this morning, and I hadn't expected him back until midafternoon.

Ozzie's wrinkles deepened. "Already? It took me hours to count, identify, and catalog all those Lladros, Hümmels, Dresden lace figurines, and even more unsigned shepherds and shepherdesses. It's precisely 4:30, according to my pocket watch."

"Four thirty!" Where had the time gone? "Oh, oh, oh, oh, oh! Gotta run. I'm supposed to set up an appointment with a new client—I hope—for later this evening, and I can't show up in these awful rags."

Ozzie took a good look and wrinkled his nose—the one part of his face not otherwise creased. "Yes, indeed, miss, you do look a fright."

No matter how much I beg, wheedle, or nag, Ozzie refuses to call me by my first name. I'm the majority partner in the business and therefore, in his fuddy-duddy, Victorian mind, require formal address. I'll never get used to it, but I try not to object anymore.

"Gee, thanks. I really needed confirmation."

"Just speaking the truth, miss, as I vowed I'd do when we signed the documents."

Ozzie has a blot or two in his past, which I discovered as a result of the untimely death of my mentor, who bequeathed me the auction house in the first place. When I offered him the partnership, he refused an equal share. He agreed to a 40 percent stake but insisted our lawyer add verbiage as to his commitment to honesty at all times, in all matters, in every way, form, or fashion, beyond a shadow of a doubt, forever and ever, till death do us part . . . you get the picture.

"Yeah, okay. I know how you value honesty, and I appreciate it. But I have to run. I'd love to land this job, even though I'll have to work with Dutch again."

Ozzie donned a knowing smile.

I squirmed.

"You two do charge the air with more power than a badly wired lamp," he said. "But you also make a lovely couple indeed."

"Couple! You're nuts, Ozzie. The guy's a menace, and I only put up with him because I wanted Noreen's job. And I want to do the Marshalls' house. They already hired him, so I'm stuck working with the . . . the . . . oh, you know what a pain he is."

More animation than I'd ever seen on him lit up Ozzie's droopy features. "I don't know, Miss Haley. There is much to be said for that certain effervescence between a man and a woman—"

I clapped my hands over my ears. "No way! I won't listen to one more word. Gotta go."

I ran out to the parking lot, jumped into my trusty Honda Civic, looped the handless gizmo for my cell phone over my head, and pulled out into the street. Thankfully, the traffic was light.

A quick call to Noreen gained me the phone number and directions to the Marshall home. Another short call set up a meeting with Deedee Marshall for the evening. But when my new potential client mentioned that Dutch would meet us there, the memory of my indignity returned with a vengeance.

I didn't want to come face-to-face with him—ever.

I stopped at a red light. As I waited, dread grew to elephantine proportions. I really, really didn't want to see Dutch Merrill again. But as the old Rolling Stones song says, you can't always get what you want—

"Aaargh!" I smacked my forehead against the steering wheel. The man was something else. The last time the song came to mind was back when he was sure I'd murdered Marge Norwalk and he wanted me jailed. Lousy memories, I'd say.

I wanted nothing to do with Dutch. But I wouldn't get what I wanted, at least not where it came to him. And I wanted the Marshall job.

The light turned green, traffic remained light, and I made it home in record time. At the Wilmont River Church's manse, I ran up the porch steps, gave Midas, my demanding golden retriever, his obligatory ear scratch, scooped clean clothes from closet and drawers, and flew to the shower. But once I found myself under the soothing warm spray, my reluctance grew.

One way or another I would have to get over my Dutch phobia. I turned to the Lord. I couldn't face the gargantuan task on my own, but I knew he alone could move mountains, create worlds, heal hearts . . . surely he could . . . oh, I don't know . . . maybe he could turn Dutch into a golden retriever of a man.

You know, friendly, always happy, eager to cooperate, quick to please.

I stepped out of the shower, and the real deal stood at the door to my room. Midas's fluffy golden tail thwacked either side of the door frame, his goofy grin spanned from ear to ear, and his beggar's brown eyes beseeched, invited me to play, conveyed his certainty that I was the best thing since faux-finish glaze in five-gallon cans.

A vision of Dutch's face popped in between Midas's long, wavy-haired ears, and I laughed. The idiotic image went a long way to ease my dread. The next time the forceful, opinionated, argumentative, stubborn, good-looking contractor gave me a hard time, all I had to do was click back to this image, and my perspective on whatever grief he was dishing should improve.

I snagged my portfolio, where I keep a ring of paint-color chips, a wide assortment of sample fabrics, a few pieces of wood with different stains, and catalogs from my favorite to-the-trades furniture manufacturers, then hurried out only to have to dash back inside for my camera and hundred-foot-long tape measure. Can't do much without those.

Then I drove to the Marshalls' ritzy address. Massive brick columns flanked open wrought-iron gates. Since the gates hung ajar and Deedee Marshall knew I was on my way, I went right on through. After what seemed like a miles-long drive up the side of the hill, I spotted the house. Three stories of red brick Georgian formality loomed at the end of the circular, white gravel drive. Black double doors wore identical brass knockers polished not so long ago—no fingerprints marred the rich gleam.

Before I used one, the right-side door opened to reveal a tall, slender blonde in head-to-toe pink silk. She was maybe thirty—no less than twenty years younger than Dr. Marshall—and wore a welcoming smile with all the pink.

"You must be Haley," she said, her voice a soft and breathy echo of Marilyn Monroe. "I'm Deedee. Come on in."

When she stepped aside, I caught my first glimpse of exquisite antique mahogany, gleaming marble, a vast gilded Victorian mirror that must have cost more than the land the manse and church sit on, and the most exquisite old Turkish Oushak rug I've ever seen.

"I don't understand." I turned another circle in the cavernous foyer. "You don't need my help. This is the most beautiful place I've ever seen."

Deedee wrinkled her nose and waved. "Stewie's ex was into all this old stuff, but I can't stand it. If it's not new, then it's not me, you know? I like exciting, contemporary styles. And I, like, can't stand these drab, dull, depressing colors."

"Okay." Wait till my nemesis heard Deedee's description of this magnificence. Dutch and I nearly came to verbal blows when he thought I harbored evil intentions for a Carrara marble fireplace mantel in Noreen's new mansion.

"So tell me, Deedee. Where would you like me to start? I have my camera and would like some pictures to start to put together a design concept for you."

"Oh, that's so cool! Let me show you the back patio." She trotted off down the center hallway, and I followed, practically drooling at the beauty I recorded with my camera along the way—these were for me. I fought to keep my attention on the trophy wife's words.

"Stewie and I want to knock down the back wall of the kitchen and dinette area so we can put full-length windows in its place."

Deedee stepped into the large kitchen in 1980s décor, then pointed to the farm-style door a bit left of center. My digital camera did its thing.

Then, with a twist of her delicate, acrylic-nailed, pink-mani-cured hand, Deedee turned the doorknob. "Let's go outside so you can see our killer view—"

A bloodcurdling shriek put an end to her words.

The Marshalls have a killer view, all right. But the view had nothing to do with the girl who lay sprawled in the middle of said patio's concrete floor, her body's lower half drenched in bright red blood.

I screamed too.

Ginny Aiken, a former newspaper reporter, lives in Pennsylvania with her engineer husband and their four sons. Born in Havana, Cuba, and raised in Valencia and Caracas, Venezuela, she discovered books at an early age. She wrote her first novel at age fifteen while she trained with the Ballets de Caracas, later to be known as the Venezuelan National Ballet. College, followed by an eclectic blend of jobs, including stints as reporter, paralegal, choreographer, language teacher, retail salesperson, wife, mother of four sons, and herder of their numerous and assorted friends, brought her back to books in search of her sanity. She is now the author of twenty published works but is still looking for that long-lost sanity.